W9-BZB-898

Sports
Camp

Sports Camp

RICH WALLACE

Alfred A. Knopf

New York

THIS IS A BORZOI BOOK PUBLISHED BY ALFRED A. KNOPF

All rights reserved. Published in the United States by Alfred A. Knopf, an imprint of Random House Children's Books, a division of Random House, Inc., New York.

Knopf, Borzoi Books, and the colophon are registered trademarks of Random House, Inc.

Visit us on the Web! www.randomhouse.com/kids

Educators and librarians, for a variety of teaching tools, visit us at . www.randomhouse.com/teachers

Library of Congress Cataloging-in-Publication Data
Wallace, Rich.
Sports camp / Rich Wallace. — 1st ed.
    p.   cm.
Summary: Eleven-year-old Riley Liston tries to fit in at Camp Olympia, a summer sports camp where he is one of the youngest boys.
ISBN 978-0-375-84059-3 (trade) — ISBN 978-0-375-94059-0 (lib. bdg.) — ISBN 978-0-375-89535-7 (e-book)
[1. Camps—Fiction. 2. Sports—Fiction. 3. Competition (Psychology)—Fiction.] I. Title.
PZ7.W15877Sp 2010
[Fic]—dc22
2009004278

The text of this book is set in 12-point Goudy.

Printed in the United States of America
April 2010
10 9 8 7 6 5 4 3 2 1
First Edition

For my parents, who sent me to camp

CHAPTER ONE
Facing the Wall

*R*iley Liston's first glimpse of the lake came as the bus wheels screeched around a tight turn on the rural highway. He could see the water shining in the sunlight beyond the trees. The driver braked hard, and Riley lunged forward. The minibus made a sharp right onto a narrow dirt road and rattled past the CAMP OLYMPIA sign.

The sign—featuring a painting of a giant snapping turtle—looked considerably shabbier than it had in the brochure. From what Riley could see of the buildings up ahead, the rest of the camp looked run-down, too.

"That thing had my foot in its mouth last year, I swear!" said Barry Monahan, the pudgy kid in the seat in front of Riley. "I've still got a scar."

"That thing" was Big Joe, the legendary resident of Lake Surprise. Said to be as wide as a wheelbarrow and as fierce as a mountain lion, the snapping turtle had been the subject of all kinds of stories from the older guys on the three-hour ride from the city. They told of kids who'd lost fingers and toes, and of others who'd barely escaped.

"About ten years ago he bit some kid's leg off!"

Riley squirmed and looked toward the lake again, but the bus had turned uphill and was approaching a ring of cabins.

When the bus stopped, a counselor stepped on board and introduced himself as Shawn. "You guys are in Cabin Three," he said.

"Who's in those other cabins?" somebody asked.

"Your rivals."

Riley swallowed hard and grabbed his backpack from the rack above his seat. He'd done well at sports in the past—Little League baseball, YMCA soccer—but he'd be one of the youngest kids at this two-week sports camp in the backwoods of Pennsylvania. Most of the guys on the bus were twelve, and a few—Barry and Hernando—had already turned thirteen. Riley's eleventh birthday had been in April.

"Move your butt," said the guy behind him as they stood in the aisle.

Riley looked back. Tony Maniglia, who towered over Riley, was smiling as if he'd been joking—there was no way Riley could go anywhere until the line started to move.

Riley could sense that these older guys would be picking on the smaller ones like him. He knew most of them from their neighborhood in Jersey City, but not well. They'd been to camp before; Riley hadn't.

The only other eleven-year-old in the group was Barry Monahan's scrawny little brother, Patrick. He wasn't much bigger than Riley, but Patrick could have kicked his butt in two seconds. Riley had seen him working in the alley behind Monahan's Tavern, lifting beer kegs that Riley wouldn't have been able to budge.

Riley took a lower bunk against the wall, below Patrick. The inside walls of the cabin had been painted a pale yellow many years before, and the floor was bare gray boards. There were also ten lockers but no locks.

Riley spread out his sleeping bag, shoved his backpack under the bunk, and hung his sweatshirt and rain jacket in the locker.

"Cabin Three . . . ," Barry was saying. "I seem to remember that this is the haunted one. I stayed in Cabin Six last year, but the guys in this one were always scared to be in here alone."

Riley looked around. It didn't look spooky in the daylight. He read the sheet of paper that had been sitting on every bunk:

CAMP OLYMPIA BULLETIN

Saturday, July 31

BASKETBALL ACTION BEGINS TONIGHT

Triple-header on Tap

> **Who:** Cabin 1 Wonders vs. Cabin 2 Tubers (Cabin 3 Threshers vs. Cabin 4 Fortunes and Cabin 5 Fighters vs. Cabin 6 Sixers to follow)
> **When:** 6:30 p.m.
> **Where:** The spacious and modern Olympia Arena
> **What's at Stake:** Team points toward the Big Joe Trophy!

Softball, Water Polo Get Under Way Tomorrow

> **Softball:** Sunday morning at the Arthur Drummond Memorial Stadium
>
> **Water Polo:** After lunch at the Lake Surprise Aquatics and Fitness Center
>
> Each camper must play at least one quarter of every basketball game and one half of each water-polo event
>
> **Upcoming:** Two-man canoe races, a cross-country running relay, the tug-of-war, and lots more, including the camp-ending Lake Surprise Showdown (a marathon swim race)

Best of luck to all Camp Olympia athletes!

Shawn, the counselor—a physical-education major from East Stroudsburg University—took them on a quick tour of the facilities. The "arena" turned out to be an old barn with a cement floor, and the "stadium" was a softball field with a chain-link backstop.

The Camp Olympia Institute for Sports Nutrition smelled greasy and kind of smoky. It consisted of long folding tables with wooden benches in a metal-sided building. Riley noticed an old sign leaning against the building and partly obscured by weeds. It said MESS HALL.

They were also shown the bathhouse and latrine, affectionately known as the Larry. Tony Maniglia, walking next to Riley, whispered, "I'm surprised they haven't renamed it the Center for the Study of Urination and Hygiene."

Dinner consisted of hamburgers, pasty mashed potatoes, and soggy green beans, gathered from a cafeteria line. After eating, they met up back at the cabin and were issued their uniforms—orange shirts with black numbers (Riley got number 5) for the basketball and softball games and matching orange sweatbands to wear for water polo and races.

Very cool, Riley thought. There was nothing like a team uniform, even if it was just a cotton T-shirt.

They walked back to the arena for their first basketball game, against Cabin 4. Shawn watched his Cabin 3 guys shoot for a few minutes and picked five players to start the game. Riley took a seat on the bench with Eldon, Kirby, Patrick, and Diego. He definitely wasn't one of the best five.

"You others stay alert," Shawn said. "You'll be out there soon."

Riley did some stretching and passed a ball back and forth with Patrick. The starters did well and built a three-point lead after one quarter. But Cabin 4 had taken an opposite strategy, putting its five least skilled players on the floor at the start to get their mandatory time over with.

So in the second quarter, Riley found himself being covered by the best point guard in the camp. He had the ball stolen the first two times he handled it and got beat three times for fast-break layups. Eldon and Kirby were totally outsized at forward. At halftime Riley's team trailed 21–12.

"You guys stink," said Vinnie Kazmerski, Cabin 3's tallest player, who'd mostly been responsible for the first-quarter lead.

"Yeah," said Barry, staring right at Riley. "You looked like you were afraid of them. We need *athletes* on this team, not wimps."

So Riley sat between Eldon and Kirby and watched the second half as his team tried in vain to overcome the deficit. They wound up losing by two.

Shawn gathered the team around him before sending them back to the cabin. "My fault," he said. "I should have paid more attention to how they were lining up."

"We'll slaughter them next time," said Barry. "In the play-offs."

"The Trading Post's open," Shawn said. "Hit the showers and hang around camp, but don't wander off. Lights-out is at eleven."

Despite the loss, guys were snapping towels and laughing in the shower room. Riley tried to face the wall the whole time. He had no muscles to speak of, and only a few thin hairs were growing anywhere besides his head.

He was scrubbing his face when the water suddenly went ice-cold, and he jumped back and opened his eyes.

Patrick was standing there with a big grin. Riley frowned and reset the faucet, then he rinsed quickly and got out of there.

His teammates set off for the Trading Post in groups of two or three. Riley followed by himself.

The Trading Post was up a steep path next to the dining hall. It was about the size of the cabins, and two counselors stood behind a counter midway through the room. Camp Olympia T-shirts and sweatshirts hung from the walls, and there were rows of candy bars and gum and a large cooler of drinks. On a table were craft items like a fat dowel with indications of where to carve a totem pole. Riley picked up a whittling knife and looked it over.

"Just get drinks," Barry Monahan was saying to his brother and some of the other guys. "We've got a stash of food at the cabin."

Riley didn't think that included him, so he bought a Crunch bar and sat at a picnic table outside in the dark to eat it. The guys from Cabin 4 had arrived, and the kid who'd eaten Riley alive in the second quarter gave him a nod.

There was some trash-talking between Barry and Vinnie and some of the players from Cabin 4; just ranting about the unfair mismatch in the second quarter and how they'd be getting revenge in the water-polo game in a few days.

But soon Riley's cabin mates were walking back. They walked right past Riley and didn't even notice he was there.

Riley could see the cabins in the distance, and he waited until he saw the Monahans and the others go inside. And even though he knew everyone in the cabin, it hit him that he didn't have any real friends at Camp Olympia.

CHAPTER TWO
Off the Path

*T*wo jumbo red and white cardboard buckets from Jersey Chicken were sitting on a bench in the middle of the cabin when Riley finally walked in. The place was famous back in their neighborhood in Jersey City; Riley and his dad went there at least twice a month to bring home a bucket. The Monahans must have picked some up and brought it with them.

Riley's mouth watered, but he didn't look into the buckets to see if there was any chicken left. Big Vinnie was licking his fingers; Barry was chawing down on a leg.

"Goo-oood," Hernando said, tossing a bone into the garbage can.

"Lights-out!" one of the counselors shouted from somewhere outside. Riley climbed into his sleeping bag.

"Story time," Barry said. "Let me fill you guys in on a little of what we're up against here."

Riley had always pegged Barry as a jerk, but he did turn out to be an especially good storyteller. He told them about the kid who disappeared from camp in the middle of the night "about fifteen or sixteen years ago." He was never seen again, but the rumor was that you could still hear him giggling in the forest late on summer nights. The laughs always ended with a terrified scream.

Things were quiet for a few minutes. The only light was from Barry's flashlight, muffled by a black T-shirt he'd placed over it.

Riley stared up at the bunk above him. Over the years, dozens of kids had carved their names or written them in pen on the wooden slats:

JOEY DIPISA, '07.
M.R. WAS HERE!
KENNY V. 2006

"Cozy sleeping quarters," Barry said. "Only thing missing is my girlfriend."

"What girlfriend?" asked his brother, Patrick.

"Any one of them would do," Barry replied. "A little making out before bedtime would be just the thing, don't you agree, Vinnie?"

"You said it," Vinnie replied.

"So how many girls have *you* made out with, Liston?"
Barry said with a laugh.

"I don't know," Riley mumbled. He'd been hoping to
stay out of this conversation.

"Can't count that high, huh, Riley boy?" Barry laughed
again, and everybody else laughed with him. "Don't worry,
twerp, it'll happen one of these years."

"Leave him alone," Tony said. "He can't help it if his
hair hasn't sprouted yet."

Riley blinked hard and rolled over to face the wall. This
could be a tough two weeks; these guys had lots more going
on than basketball. He was the smallest kid in the cabin,
maybe in the whole camp. He threw back the top of his
sleeping bag and sat up. He pulled on a pair of shorts and his
sneakers, picked up his flashlight, and headed for the door.

"Where you going?" Barry asked.

"To the bathroom."

He slipped outside. A light was on in the counselors'
cabin, but no one was around. Riley followed the path toward the latrine, but he had a different destination. In the
distance he could see a single lightbulb burning by the boat
house, so he quietly made his way down the hill toward
the lake.

A breeze was coming off the water, and it smelled faintly
of fish and algae and weeds.

11

They'd been warned that any camper caught in the water or on the dock after hours would be sent home, so Riley followed a narrow, wooded path along the shore.

The lake wasn't huge—about three-quarters of a mile long and a quarter mile wide—but it was dark and said to be deep. It could get choppy in a hurry when a storm came up.

Riley walked slowly, keeping his hand over the flashlight beam so he wouldn't attract attention. The path seemed to circle the entire lake, but he had no intention of doing the whole loop at night. There were bears in the woods and probably snakes, and maybe that creepy missing kid, too. And one wrong turn would have certainly got him lost.

So he stopped about a hundred yards past the dock and stepped to the edge of the lake. The moon was high in the sky, but it was only a crescent, so it wasn't providing much light.

"I'm not *that* bad at basketball," he said to himself, barely above a whisper. It wasn't his best sport, that was for sure, but he could dribble. He could outshoot his father sometimes when they played one-on-one in the driveway at home. With a more reasonable matchup than tonight's, he could play good defense.

He knew he'd do better at water polo—he was a strong

swimmer—and would probably hold his own in softball. But tonight's game had been a setback, for sure. The rest of the guys in the cabin already considered him a weakling.

He thought about that marathon swim race, the last night of camp. The length of the lake and back. Swimming for nearly an hour. Not just swimming, but *racing*. He could do that.

He'd been swimming since he was two.

But that race was a long way off. Almost two whole weeks. Two solid weeks of crappy food, group showers, Barry's stupid insults, and—worst of all—nobody his age to hang around with.

"Geronimo!"

A shout back at the dock made him look that way with a start. In the dim light from the boat house he could see several of the counselors. One of them dove off the dock and the others jumped in, too. They started tossing a water-polo ball around, slapping at the water and laughing.

He'd surely be seen if he walked past the dock. Nobody said he couldn't *walk* by the lake at night, but he was pretty sure he wasn't supposed to. Certainly not after lights-out, when the only excuse for leaving the cabin was to use the bathroom.

And he was getting very sleepy. The only choice he had was to walk around the lake—either that or make a roundabout circuit through the woods to avoid the dock. But the terrain on this side of the lake was steep and rocky, and there was no way he could leave the path without shining his flashlight. That'd be a dead giveaway, too.

So Riley set off on the path again, praying that it would bring him all the way around the lake.

Stupid, he thought. *Why didn't you just stay put and go to sleep?*

The walk was easy until he reached the far end of the lake and started to loop around the edge. Then the footing began to get mucky, and suddenly he'd reached the brook that provided the lake's outlet. Somehow he'd gone off the path.

"No!" he said in frustration.

The brook was about ten feet wide where it exited the lake, but seemed to narrow as it moved farther downstream. The woods were thickest down at this end, and Riley was scared.

He looked back down the lake. The counselors were still in the water near the dock, and from this vantage point Riley could see other lights—at the dining hall and the Larry and the gym. They seemed very far away.

He slapped at a mosquito and felt it squash against his neck.

Somewhere out in that lake a giant snapping turtle

waited patiently, perhaps for a bass to swim by. Maybe for a camper.

Riley followed the brook, shining his light fully now. He breathed a sigh of relief as the light caught his escape route—a simple wooden bridge about thirty yards down-stream. He could also see where the path resumed on the opposite side.

He rapped his fist against his thigh and stepped onto the bridge. It was sturdy. He'd be back in bed in fifteen minutes.

The path was wider on this side of the lake and less bumpy. The moon was higher now and the sky was clear, so he shut off the flashlight and walked more carefully. He stumbled a couple of times but didn't fall, and soon he was climbing the grassy hill that led to the open area between the cabins.

Everyone seemed to be asleep. Riley pulled open the squeaky screen door and waited for his eyes to adjust to the darker room. Then he sat on his bunk and took off his sneakers.

Patrick Monahan peeked over the edge of the top bunk at him. "That must have been some long whiz."

"I just wanted some air. I was looking at the stars for a while."

"See any UFOs?"

"Not even an airplane. No ghosts yet, huh?"

"Not one. Eldon threw up."

"When?"

"About a half hour ago."

"In here?"

"No. He got outside. Over by the woods."

"Oh."

Riley crawled into his sleeping bag. Barry was snoring, but everything else was peaceful.

Eldon was a year ahead of Riley in school. He was on a lower bunk across the way. Riley looked over and could see that Eldon was looking back.

"I felt sick ever since that bus ride," Eldon said. "That greasy hamburger didn't help any."

"You better now?"

"Much. I'll sleep it off."

Barry let out a big snorty snore and sat up. "Hey, everybody shut up, huh? Some of us are trying to sleep."

"You shut up," said Patrick. "You sound like a buzz saw."

"I'll buzz-saw your head in a minute if you don't shut your face. Hey, look, the wanderer is back."

Riley knew Barry was referring to him.

"Where'd you go?" Barry continued.

"The bathroom."

"What'd you do, fall in? You were gone like an hour."

"Just hanging around," Riley said.

"Like a night crawler."

Then Barry started talking about Cabin 3.

"As long as we're up," he said, "let me tell you why you all might think twice about venturing outside by yourself at night. I'll tell you what went down in this very cabin last summer, but it happens all over camp. The ghostly stuff, I mean.

"What happened in here wasn't any violent haunting or anything like that," he said slowly. "Just this feeling of being watched, of being an intruder in this spirit's domain. One guy told me he woke up at about two-thirty and saw this phantom floating above his bunk—a misty, glowing shape with wide, dark eyes looking right at him. The guy had to go to the Larry, but he held it until the next morning, too scared to even move. The thing just drifted away or dissolved, but the kid said he never slept more than fifteen minutes at a time the whole rest of camp.

"Other guys had similar experiences. They swore it was true. I believed 'em."

They fell into silence, and within a minute Barry was snoring again. Riley lay awake for quite some time, staring straight up with his hands behind his head.

He'd been hoping everyone would be sleeping when he got back and not aware of how long he was gone, but obviously they'd noticed. Then again, that was probably better than if they hadn't.

He was safe now, but that had been a pretty cool adventure.

The Wanderer. The Night Crawler.

Having a nickname or two was a start toward fitting in, at least.

CAMP OLYMPIA BULLETIN
Sunday, August 1

LATE BASKET LIFTS FIGHTERS TO VICTORY

Wonders and Fortunes Also Win

Danny Avila's baseline jumper at the buzzer capped a furious comeback Saturday night as the Cabin 5 Fighters edged the Cabin 6 Sixers, 33–32, at the Olympia Arena. Trailing 27–20 after three quarters, the Fighters utilized a patient inside game to whittle away at the lead. Avila finished with 13 points.

Other scores: Cabin 1 Wonders 38, Cabin 2 Tubers 25; Cabin 4 Fortunes 37, Cabin 3 Threshers 35

Practice That J Stroke; Canoe Race Is Coming!

Two-man teams from every cabin will vie for the first major championship of this camp season on Monday afternoon in the 600-meter canoe race. Each cabin can enter three teams.

Sure, It's a Sport! Karaoke Contest Is Tonight

Camp Olympia athletes are known for their powerful biceps and quadriceps, but who has the camp's strongest vocal cords? We'll find out tonight at the All-Star Karaoke and Dance Contest. Each cabin can enter two teams of up to four participants. Judging will be by camp staff.

Where: Olympia Center for Music and Culture

When: 8 p.m.

What's at Stake: Team points toward the Big Joe Trophy!

Some Rules to Live By

—No visits to the lake unless a counselor is present.

—No seconds on anything unless you've eaten everything on your plate.

—"Lights-out" means go to sleep!

CHAPTER THREE
Below the Surface

*R*iley plunged off the wooden dock into the murky green water and let himself sink. Underwater, the visibility was near zero; just a few rays of sunlight broke through and turned streaks of the lake a paler green.

Riley's left foot reached the bottom of soft, slimy vegetation and he pushed off, breaking the surface and inhaling.

The water felt great: warm on the top layer and much cooler a few feet below. Riley started swimming, headed for the small floating dock about fifty yards out. Several campers and a counselor were already there.

The swimming area was marked with ropes and floats. A second area for water polo was on one side of the main dock, and the camp's canoes and rowboats were tethered to the other.

Riley quickly reached the floating dock and hauled

himself up. He had about fifteen minutes before the water-polo match. Cabin 3 had already played its softball game, managing a 9–6 win. Riley had been stuck in right field the whole game, but he hadn't made any errors. He hadn't had any hits either.

"You're supposed to have a buddy," the counselor on the floating dock said.

"A what?"

"A buddy. No camper is allowed off the main dock unless he's buddied up with someone. Next time you swim out here, you need to have someone with you."

That was news to Riley. He loved to swim, but most of his cabin mates were doing cannonballs off the main dock or just splashing around in the shallow water. Riley wanted to swim laps.

"Does it have to be somebody from my cabin?" he asked.

"No. Anybody. Any *buddy*." The counselor laughed as if he'd said something hilarious.

Riley would have to find someone. He'd been on a competitive swim team for the past two winters at the YMCA. Most of the races were short—25 or 50 meters—but the training was rigorous. Swimming nonstop for a half hour or so wasn't a big deal for him. He enjoyed it.

He looked across the water toward the main dock. "Can I swim *back* alone?" he asked.

"Yeah, go ahead. I'll keep an eye on you."

So Riley took his time heading across, stroking out to the middle of the swimming area before curling over to the dock. It gave him a few minutes to think about the other nine guys in his cabin. Would any of them want to be his "buddy"?

—*Fat Barry Monahan*. Great storyteller and a great sense of humor, but Riley could tell that he looked down on him as a scrawny little kid.

—*Patrick Monahan*. Sarcastic and fidgety. Who'd want to be his buddy, anyway?

—*Vinnie Kazmerski*. Too old for Riley to hang out with. Too big. Too full of himself.

—*Hernando Valenzuela*. Funny and strong. And a lot like Vinnie.

—*Tony Maniglia*. Part of the Barry-Vinnie-Hernando crowd, but a nice kid when he was on his own.

—*Eldon Johnson*. Quiet. Almost a year older than Riley, but he seemed like a good guy.

—*Kirby Lincoln*. Didn't seem very bright or athletic or talkative or friendly.

—*Colin Dugan*. Tried hard to be part of the Barry crowd. Didn't seem to be succeeding at it.

—*Diego Martinez*. Vinnie's shadow.

Riley never minded being a loner back home. There were lots of kids around to play football or street hockey with, and he was always getting into a game. When it was over, nobody took much notice when he went his own way. Here at camp it'd be different. "Going home" meant back to the cabin with nine other guys, not the easy feeling of being home with his parents.

Instead of reading a comic book in his own bed at night or just looking out the window at the New York City skyline across the river, he'd have to deal with Barry's mocking and Vinnie's bragging and anybody else's showboating.

Still, he was glad to be here. Sports were his passion. That's why he'd signed up for this camp.

Riley climbed onto the dock. The rest of Cabin 3 was warming up in the water-polo area, throwing the ball around. Shawn, the counselor, waved them over.

"Listen up," Shawn said, addressing the team. "You all got your headbands?"

Riley had his orange band looped three times around his wrist.

"Okay," Shawn said. "We play seven at a time—four forwards, two defenders, and a goalie. You can only dunk the guy who's playing the ball, so no jerking around or it'll be a penalty. And no two-on-one dunking either. That's illegal."

The water in this area was about six feet deep, so they'd be treading or swimming most of the time. The goalie and defenders could hang on to the dock when the ball was down at the other end.

The area of play was about twenty yards long and nearly as wide. Shawn put Riley on defense with Eldon, and he put Tony Maniglia in goal.

"Signal with your hand or something if you get a cramp and need to come out," Shawn said. "Or you can rest on the bottom if you want," he added with a smile.

Their opponents from Cabin 1 had green headbands and some big players. "They're from Brooklyn," Barry remarked. "They think they're pretty tough."

"We'll see about that," said Vinnie. "Let's go!"

The Cabin 3 Threshers went on the attack immediately, with Vinnie and Hernando both taking hard close-range shots in the opening minutes that were blocked by the goalie. The Brooklyn team had some less disciplined players who fired shots at Tony from well back. Tony easily caught them and tossed the ball to Barry near the center.

So Riley calmly treaded water for several minutes as he and Eldon hung back on defense, not getting any action. Finally a Cabin 1 player came racing toward the goal on a breakaway, churning through the water with the ball skimming between his arms.

The guy was big. He already had the faint beginnings of a mustache.

"Need help!" Riley called.

He darted forward, but his arms were much shorter than his opponent's, so the other player managed to dunk Riley with one hand and continue stroking with the other. Riley flapped his arms to drop lower in the water, getting free from the guy's hand and popping up a few feet away.

He spit out a mouthful and took another stroke toward the ball carrier.

Eldon had come over, too, and between the two defenders they managed to stop the attack. With Vinnie and Barry converging, the Cabin 1 player threw an off-balance shot that went wide of the goal. Tony grabbed the ball and looked around.

Riley backstroked a bit and caught Eldon's eye. He motioned with his head, and Eldon swam back to his side of the defensive zone. Two Brooklyn players had moved into that area. If their teammate had passed instead of shooting, they would have had an unguarded path to the goal.

"Nice work!" Tony said. "Good D." He threw the ball ahead to Vinnie, who immediately turned and shot.

"Too far out!" Tony yelled as the ball was caught. "Do some passing, boys."

The scoreless battle continued for several more minutes. Another long, easily blocked shot came flying to Tony from the Cabin 1 end, and Tony quickly tossed the ball to Riley.

It was his first touch of the game, and there were several

yards of open water ahead of him. He stroked toward the middle, keeping his head up as a mob of opponents swam toward him.

Riley treaded his legs hard, lifting the ball with one hand and rising up as if to shoot. Just as two opponents were almost upon him, he tossed the ball to Barry, halfway to the goal and wide open.

Barry feigned a shot and flipped the ball to Vinnie, who had a dead-on angle at the goal. He threw it high and hard, past the reaching arm of the goaltender and into the net.

"Yes!" shouted Barry, smacking the water.

The Cabin 3 players swam back to their end.

"Great pass, fat boy!" said Vinnie, punching Barry on the shoulder.

"*Two* great passes!" said Tony. "Smart work!"

By halftime, they were exhausted. Riley climbed onto the dock with the others and sprawled flat on his back.

"You'll be out for now, but stay ready," Shawn told him. "You did a great job."

Cabin 1 started to dominate in the second half. Patrick Monahan had taken over Riley's spot on the defensive end, and he was not a strong swimmer. Vinnie had moved into the goalie position, and he got bombarded with shots. The score was soon tied.

Midway through the half, Shawn sent Riley back into

27

the water. "Sub for Eldon," he said. "Keep up the strong defense, but don't be afraid to attack. We need another goal!"

So Riley watched for an opportunity. Hernando took a long shot that was deflected and spun to an open side of the Cabin 1 defensive zone. Riley reacted quickly and raced toward the ball. Barry, Hernando, and two defenders were in pursuit as well.

Straining with every stroke, Riley reached the ball first, but he knew he'd be going under. He hugged the ball tight as a strong pair of hands pushed his shoulders down. Riley kicked to try to get free, but the buoyancy of the ball prevented him from going deeper.

Suddenly the defender let Riley go, and he scrambled up to see that Hernando had dunked the guy. Riley stroked toward the center as two more opponents swam toward him. Tony, now on offense, was open to the right of the goal, waving his arms.

Riley faked left, then threw the ball to Tony. His shot bonked off the side of the goal and fell to the water several feet in front. As the goalie lunged toward it, Barry swooped in and flicked the ball over his head and into the net. Cabin 3 had taken the lead!

"How much time?" Riley called to Shawn as he swam back.

"About three minutes," Shawn called. "Defense!"

With a big surge of energy, Riley moved toward the Cabin 1 player who was bringing up the ball. Barry got there first, putting the guy under and taking control of the ball.

On the attack again, Cabin 3 finally got some teamwork going and passed the ball effectively. The ball came to Riley, then back to Hernando, then over to Tony.

Clearly frustrated, the Cabin 1 players chased after the ball. They seemed more tired than Riley's team, and time was running out. Tony fired a high, hard shot toward the corner of the goal, and the ball landed solidly in the back of the net.

Fist up, Riley let out a deep breath. This game was theirs now, and he'd played a big role. The whistle blew, and they climbed out of the water with a victory.

The sun was overhead, and there was barely a cloud. Dinner was several hours away.

"Into the boats!" shouted Barry. "Time to catch some bass."

Several of them had brought fishing gear. They hurried to the other side of the dock and signed up for boats. A lot of rowboats and canoes were already out on the lake, with pairs or trios in orange life vests.

Riley stood aside as the Monahans and Vinnie climbed into one boat; Hernando, Kirby, and Eldon into another; and Tony, Colin, and Diego into the third.

The boats shoved off, with the campers whooping and laughing about their big win. Barry slapped the lake with an oar and sent a splash of water into Tony's boat, but nobody cared. They were already wet from the game.

Riley sat on the dock to watch them go, hanging his feet in the water and feeling the warm sun on his shoulders.

He'd played well. He knew that much.

CAMP OLYMPIA BULLETIN

Monday, August 2

THRESHERS SPLASH TO WATER-POLO WIN

Cabin 3 Snares a Softball Victory, Too

The Cabin 3 Threshers racked up a pair of wins Sunday, dunking Cabin 1 in water polo and edging Cabin 6 in softball. The Threshers were the only cabin to win games in both sports.

Tony Maniglia smashed a home run and a double in the Threshers 9–6 softball win. He also had a goal in the 3–1 water-polo victory.

Other softball scores were Cabin 4 Fortunes 8, Cabin 2 Tubers 5, and Cabin 5 Fighters 11, Cabin 1 Wonders 4. Danny Avila—the star of the camp so far—had two home runs for the Fighters.

In water polo, it was Sixers 5, Fortunes 3, and Tubers 7, Fighters 5.

Tuber Talent Forges Early Lead in Points Race

A rousing rendition of "My Sharona" by Cabin 2's Phillip Lopez and Ryan McDonald capped an energetic and wildly entertaining karaoke competition Sunday night. The duo rang up a perfect 30, getting scores of 10 from each of the three judges. That result put the Tubers in the lead for the Big Joe Trophy with 6 points.

Burrrrrrrrrrp alert: *Hot-Dog-Eating Contest Is Tuesday night!*

More Rules to Live By

—No food in the cabins. (Let's not feed the mice.)

—Three people in a rowboat is the max. Two is the minimum.

—Do not carve your name into your bunk or the walls.

—Obey all rules!

CHAPTER FOUR
Bad Blood

*R*iley froze in his tracks, gazing skyward as the softball sailed high into the outfield. The arc would take it beyond where he was standing, so Riley started running, trying to keep his eye on the ball.

This could be bad. The Cabin 3 Threshers were protecting a one-run lead in the bottom of the final inning, but Cabin 5 had two men on base and that ball was heading for the fence.

Riley pushed harder, opening his stride and lifting his glove. Suddenly Vinnie's voice stopped him cold.

"I got it!" Vinnie yelled. He'd run over from center field to make the catch for the third out, securing the victory. Riley ducked out of his way and went sprawling onto the grass.

Vinnie leaped into the air and threw the ball wildly

toward the infield. The rest of the Threshers met him behind second base and mobbed him. Riley caught up and smacked gloves with Diego and Kirby.

"We're number one!" shouted Hernando. His teammates picked up the chant.

"We're number one! We're number one!"

"Get a grip," Shawn said with a laugh as they reached the bench. "There's a long way to go before anyone gives us a trophy."

"They might as well start engraving our names on it," Barry said. "We're the best team in camp."

Riley nodded. He'd had a good day—no errors again (he'd fielded several grounders and caught one pop fly) and he'd hit the ball twice (for outs) and struck out once.

"Looks like you guys got lucky," one of the players from Cabin 4 said to Barry. Cabin 4 was warming up for the next game. That was the team that had beaten the Threshers in the opening-night basketball game.

"Not as lucky as you guys were," Barry said. "We'll see you in a few days for water polo. Hope you like the taste of lake water."

"I'm scared," the guy said. "Look at me; I'm shaking."

Barry just turned and started walking toward the cabin. Most of his teammates followed.

Riley noticed that Eldon was sitting on the bench with his shoe off.

"Had a pebble in there since about the fourth inning," Eldon said. He shook out his shoe and put it back on.

Since everyone else was gone, Riley finally had somebody to walk with.

Eldon was a few inches taller than Riley and almost a year older, but he didn't quite seem to fit in with the guys his own age. He tried to join them when they bragged about girls or joked around about how tough they all were, but he spent of lot of time lying on his bunk reading comic books or sports novels, and Riley'd noticed that he always made a point of eating his vegetables and drinking all his milk.

"That was close," Eldon said. "I thought that last ball was gone."

"Me too, and I was right there." Riley shook his head. "I almost collided with Vinnie."

Eldon let out his breath in a huff. "Vinnie," he said with a bit of disgust. "These guys are *so* full of themselves. Vinnie, Barry, Hernando—they act like they own the camp or something."

Riley just shrugged. He could see that for himself, but it didn't seem like a good idea to bring it up.

Eldon stopped walking and grabbed Riley's arm. "Don't tell them I said nothing."

"I wouldn't."

"I mean, they aren't *so* bad. Just, you know . . . Believe me, Barry doesn't have a girlfriend. No way."

"I didn't figure he did," Riley said. "But I didn't feel like getting beat up the other night if I said anything."

"*That* he could do." Eldon picked up a small stone. "Think I could hit the lake from here?"

Riley looked down the hill. They were about eighty yards above the path that he'd taken on Saturday night when he walked around the lake alone. "Doubt it."

"I'll give it a shot anyway." Eldon ran a couple of steps forward and flung the stone as far as he could. It reached the line of trees but fell quite a bit short of the water.

"Not bad," Riley said.

"Maybe if I used a heavier rock." But Eldon didn't look for another. He rubbed his shoulder instead. "Maybe not . . . So what are we doing?"

"Now?"

"Yeah," Eldon said. "We got at least an hour to kill before dinner."

"I don't know. Could check out the Trading Post again."

"I been there ten times. You buy me a candy bar?"

"Okay." Riley reached into his pocket and felt for the dollar bill he kept there. That would get two candy bars. He could spare it.

But then they saw Barry walking toward them, waving his arms. "Get over here!" he called.

"What's up?" Eldon yelled back.

"We've been sabotaged! Get your butts to the cabin."

Eldon broke into a run and Riley followed.

The inside of the cabin looked like something out of a horror movie. Green slime was dripping down the walls, and socks and T-shirts had been pulled from some of the lockers and thrown around the cabin. A pile of garbage—greasy napkins, corncobs, banana peels—was sitting on top of Barry's sleeping bag. And on the wall above Vinnie's bunk were the words GET OUT in black writing.

"Ghosts?" Eldon asked.

"Idiots," Barry said. "It had to be those jerks from Cabin Four."

"What about that slime?" Patrick asked, pointing to the wall. "It looks like ectoplasm!"

Barry stepped over and rubbed the green stuff with a finger. He sniffed it and gave out a humorless laugh. "Shampoo," he said. "Apple or lime, I believe. And that"—he pointed to the GET OUT notation—"was written with a burnt stick. There's ghosts in this cabin—I'm not denying that—but this is plain old bad blood."

"So what are we gonna do about it?" Hernando said, pounding his fist into his hand.

Barry gave Hernando a sinister look, then smiled thoughtfully. "Bide our time. Act like we have no idea how this could have happened. We'll get even and then some. Just let me think it over for a few days."

Barry looked around at the walls, then pointed to Riley

and Eldon. "You two twerps!" he said. "Hit the Larry and bring back some wet paper towels. Some dry ones, too."

They started straightening up the cabin. It didn't take long. Barry hung his sleeping bag over a fence railing in the sunlight to rid it of the trash smell, and Eldon wiped the sooty message off the wall.

"Not a word to anybody," Barry said. "Not even the counselors. We'll handle this in our own way, and it *will* be sweet."

"We should wait until they're at a basketball game or something, then mess up Cabin Four twice as bad as this one," Vinnie said.

"Get deer crap from the woods and smear it on their walls," said Patrick.

"Catch some snakes and put them in their bunks," said Hernando.

"Don't worry," Barry said. "We can do a lot better than this." He opened his palm and gestured around the cabin. "A stunt like they pulled takes very little creativity. When we get our revenge, it'll be *spectacular*."

CAMP OLYMPIA BULLETIN
Wednesday, August 4

CABIN 6 PADDLERS DOMINATE RACE

Canoe Points Give Sixers Overall Lead

The Cabin 6 team of Troy Hiller and Avery Moretti captured the two-man canoe race on Tuesday, edging the Sullivan-Singh boat from Cabin 2. The Sixers picked up more points with a third-place finish.

Cabin 6 is leading the race toward the Big Joe Trophy, despite being winless in basketball and softball. The big points in those sports and water polo will be awarded after the playoffs.

Monahan Is Top Dog in Eating Contest

Cabin 3 sensation Barry Monahan flabbergasted the experts Tuesday night, downing 13 hot dogs in 15 minutes to knock off defending champion Luis Vega of Cabin 5. Vega, trailing early, roared back in the final minutes and closed with 12 dogs, one better than he did a year ago. But that wasn't enough to overcome Monahan, who said he could have eaten more, "but I didn't like the mustard they put on the dogs."

Standings

Basketball	W	L
Cabin 4	2	0
Cabin 5	2	0
Cabin 1	1	1
Cabin 2	1	1
Cabin 3	0	2
Cabin 6	0	2

Softball	W	L
Cabin 3	2	0
Cabin 4	1	1
Cabin 1	1	1
Cabin 2	1	1
Cabin 5	1	1
Cabin 6	0	2

Water Polo	W	L
Cabin 2	2	0
Cabin 3	2	0
Cabin 4	1	1
Cabin 6	1	1
Cabin 1	0	2
Cabin 5	0	2

Total Points

Cabin 6	20
Cabin 2	19
Cabin 3	12
Cabin 1	11
Cabin 5	11
Cabin 4	5

CHAPTER FIVE
Big Joe's First Victim

*I*t was just about fully dark, and the Monahan brothers had a fire going in the metal trash barrel behind the cabin. Barry had thrown in a long damp branch of green pine, so sparks and smoke were shooting into the air.

Riley had just brushed his teeth over at the bathhouse and was taking the long way around when Barry caught sight of him and called him over. "Hey, Night Crawler!"

"What?" Riley asked. He was still wary around Barry. He never knew what the guy might pull.

Barry gestured toward the barrel. "Warm your hands," he said. "It feels good."

"I'm plenty warm." But Riley stood by the barrel and held out his palms just to seem friendly.

"The smoke keeps the bugs away," Patrick said. "So, that was another awful dinner, huh?"

Riley rolled his eyes. They'd had salmon croquettes and mushy carrots. He'd tried to fill up on bread, but everybody else'd had the same idea and there wasn't any extra. So he bought a Milky Way at the Trading Post after the basketball game—they'd finally got a win—but he wasn't satisfied.

Patrick pointed his thumb toward the cabin. "We still got a stash."

"Candy?"

"Chicken."

Riley's eyes opened wide. "You still have that Jersey Chicken from *Saturday?*"

"It's all good," Patrick said. "You'll see." He tossed a handful of pinecones into the barrel and went inside the cabin. He came back with a black trash bag and pulled out the remaining red and white bucket. A soiled gray sock came out, too.

"Your laundry?" Riley asked.

"Some of it. I figured the dampness would help keep the chicken moist. Don't worry, I kept the lid on the bucket."

The bucket still held a small breast, a wing, and a couple of thighs. "I threw some ice in the bag on Monday, too, to keep it fresh," Patrick said. "And it's been in my locker all this time, out of the heat."

Riley peered into the bucket and sniffed. The heavily breaded chicken didn't smell fresh, but it didn't smell rotten either.

"Have some," Patrick said, taking a bite out of one of the thighs. "It's still okay. We been eating it every night."

Riley took the wing. The skin was slick and the meat was dried out, but it had that unmistakable Jersey Chicken flavor, salty and peppery and a little garlicky. He gnawed it right down to the bones: skin, cartilage, gristle—it all tasted good. The best thing he'd eaten all week.

"Take the last one," Patrick said. "You had the smallest piece."

"You sure?"

"Yeah. We're tired of Jersey Chicken anyway. We've had it five nights in a row."

"A man can only eat so much chicken," Barry said. "And so many hot dogs."

So Riley ate the last thigh and Patrick dumped the bucket and the bones into the barrel.

Though they weren't very good at basketball, the Monahans had proven to be the nucleus of the Cabin 3 softball team. Barry—he seemed to be cool with having the guys refer to him as Fat Barry, though Riley wouldn't dare—was a good first baseman and a power hitter. And Patrick was quick and wiry and could hit anything thrown at him. The brothers were the main reason they'd won their first two games.

A few other kids had wandered over and the moon was up in the sky, so Barry launched into one of his horror stories. "This one happened right in these woods," he began, speaking slowly and staring at the fire, "oh, about sixty years ago. Way before this was a camp. Before there was even a paved road through these parts of the county . . ."

The chicken bucket ignited, and the orange glow lit up the other faces. Eldon and Kirby. Riley looked around. He could see the Big Dipper low in the sky over to the west. There were lights on in most of the cabins.

"There'd been a fight," Barry was saying. "You guys might have seen that old run-down barn on the left about a mile south of here; we passed it on the way in. That farm's been out of business for decades. Anyway, they say one of the hands—Maynard, they called him—got in an argument with the farmer about his wages. . . ."

Riley's eyes met Eldon's straight across the barrel, and Eldon looked away. Somebody shouted way over near the latrine. Just a name. Arnie or Harvey, something like that.

"The farmer heard a noise in the kitchen that night and rushed down the stairs to see Maynard slipping out the door. It seemed obvious that he'd been there to steal what he thought was rightfully his. So the farmer and his son took off after him. Maynard ran into the woods."

Riley felt a surge of energy. And maybe fear. Those woods were dark. Must have been a whole lot darker back then.

"It was a pitch-black night; you could barely see the ground in front of you. Maynard's all scratched up from branches hitting his face, but he keeps running like his life is on the line. The farmer's got a torch, so Maynard knows he's getting closer. He also knows the farmer's got a gun!"

Kirby let out a nervous laugh. Patrick picked up another piece of punky wood and dropped it into the barrel. More sparks shot up. And smoky warmth.

"Maynard's sense of smell was vivid, so he knew he was approaching the lake. *Our* lake. Lake Surprise. He could smell the algae and the mud and even the fish beneath the water. This guy's sense of smell was like a hunting dog's!

"He dives into the lake and starts swimming. He's puffing so hard from running through the woods that he's swallowing water with every stroke, but he presses on. The farmer and his son stop when they reach the water and fire a few shots, but they've lost sight of Maynard. They can't swim. He's getting away."

Riley licked his lips and tasted chicken grease. Everyone around the fire was wide-eyed. Barry rocked slowly back and forth as he spoke, never taking his eyes off the flames.

"After twenty minutes of swimming, Maynard's approaching the far end of the lake, that *deep* cold area that leads into the cove. He's got barely enough strength left to hold on, but in two hundred yards he'll be out of the water and on his way. In daylight he can make his way through the forest, all the way over to the Delaware River and Narrowsburg, and he'll catch a ride and be in New York City by the following afternoon with a couple of hundred stolen dollars in his pocket."

Barry's hand darted out and grabbed Riley's arm, clamping down hard. "Like *that*! Swift and sharp, Maynard feels an unbelievable pain below his elbow."

Riley jumped back. He glanced around, but everybody else had their eyes fixed on Barry, not even blinking.

Barry continued. "He takes another stroke, but there's nothing there to propel him through the water. Half his arm is gone!

"A second bite rips deep into his thigh and pulls him under the surface. He's thrashing with his good arm and leg and comes up gasping for air, the water turning red with his blood. Then the fatal blow—this massive gray head surges through the water, clamping its beak in the center of Maynard's throat and snapping right through the neck. Maynard's final thoughts are only of the pain as he sinks beneath the surface for the last time."

Barry nodded solemnly and cleared his throat. "Big Joe's first victim . . . It wasn't pretty.

"But that's not the end of the story. Not by a long shot. You'll never hear the counselors mention this—they don't want to scare anybody—but you can still hear Maynard running frantically through these woods some August nights. You'll hear the splash and swear somebody's swimming for his life across Lake Surprise around midnight, and if you listen carefully, you'll hear the crunching of his bones and his painful screams as Maynard turns into snapping-turtle prey.

"Don't get in his way when he's running—he'll knock you down and trample you. Might even drag you into the lake with him."

Barry took a deep breath and let it go. "Yeah, I heard him with my own ears last summer. A night just like this one—really quiet, really dark."

Barry shook his head and winced. He took a piece of paper towel from his pocket and tore it into a small square. He picked up a small handful of dried-out pine needles from the ground and rolled them tightly into the paper, then held the end of his homemade cigarette against the flame. He took a deep drag and held the smoke in his mouth, then handed the butt to Patrick.

The butt went around the circle. When it reached Riley, it was only about an inch long. He put it to his lips and inhaled, then started to sputter and cough. Riley quickly handed it back to Barry and rubbed his hot fingers together. They smelled like smoky pine, and his eyes were watering. Barry laughed.

Nobody said much after that; they just stared at the fire. A couple of times Riley glanced nervously toward the woods. The fire got low, and a few mosquitoes buzzed around.

Riley felt an uncomfortable gurgling in his stomach. He burped up a sour chicken taste and looked toward the latrine. He still had his toothbrush and toothpaste in his pocket.

"Must be after eleven," Kirby finally said. "What happened to 'lights-out'?"

"The third basketball game must have gone into overtime," Patrick replied.

"Maybe they just forgot," Barry said. "Maybe Maynard got 'em all."

Riley laughed. He was tired, and the qualifying for the big swim was tomorrow. But then he burped again and had to swallow some bile. Suddenly he had a bigger concern than sleep to deal with. He needed to get to the bathroom in a hurry.

That chicken hadn't been so fresh after all.

CAMP OLYMPIA BULLETIN
Thursday, August 5

SIXERS SCORE MAJOR HOOPS UPSET

Basketball Loss Is First for Fortunes

The previously winless Sixers took to the hard court Wednesday evening against the previously undefeated Cabin 4 Fortunes. Guess what? Lionel Robertson came alive for 17 points as the Sixers walked away with a 33–26 shocker.

"We're ready to roll now," Robertson said after the game. "We're not conceding that Big Joe Trophy to anybody."

In other action, the Cabin 5 Fighters remained unbeaten with a 39–27 win over the Cabin 2 Tubers. The Cabin 3 Threshers edged Cabin 1, 31–29.

Big Swim Qualifying Is This Afternoon

Twenty swimmers will earn their way into the camp-ending Lake Surprise Showdown this afternoon. The Showdown, a grueling 1.2-mile marathon swim, is set for Friday evening, August 13. In past years, points from the swim race have often decided the overall team champion.

Today's qualifying heats will cover about three-quarters of a mile, beginning at the dock and turning at the yellow buoy midway up the lake.

Two cabins at a time will swim this afternoon, with Cabins 1 and 2 starting at 1:15 p.m., 3 and 4 at 2:00, and 5 and 6 at 2:45. The twenty fastest swimmers will advance to next Friday's race.

Upcoming

Tug-of-war (Saturday morning). *Flex those muscles!*

Shuffleboard tournament (Saturday afternoon). *Sharpen your aim!*

Cross-country relay (Sunday afternoon). *Don't overeat at lunch!*

CHAPTER SIX
Orange and Brown

*R*iley stepped out of the latrine, where he'd been living since last night. There couldn't possibly be any of that rancid chicken left in his system.

He'd had no breakfast. No lunch. And the qualifying round for the big swim race was less than an hour away.

Shawn was walking toward him. He'd taken Riley to the camp nurse that morning, and she'd given him a big pink dose of Pepto-Bismol and told him to take a nap. So Riley had slept through the softball game, which Cabin 3 managed to win despite being short one outfielder.

"Any better, Liston?" Shawn asked, grinning.

Riley shrugged. "One last blast," he said. "I think that's the end of it."

"Too bad it had to happen today," Shawn said. "You had a good chance of qualifying."

"I'm still swimming," Riley said. "I can do it."

"You haven't eaten anything."

"I'm starting to feel hungry. That has to be a good sign, right?"

Shawn looked Riley over and put his palm across his forehead. He tilted his own head from side to side, thinking. "Okay. *If* you eat something and *if* it stays down. And if you start feeling the slightest bit shaky, you get right into a boat. You hear me?"

"Yeah. What can I eat?"

Shawn made a "come with me" gesture with his hand and led Riley to the counselors' cabin. "Crackers, peanut butter, fruit. Eat whatever you want. We got pretzels and chips, too. Just don't overdo it."

"I won't." Riley spread peanut butter on six Ritz crackers and ate them one at a time. Then he peeled an orange and ate that.

"Thanks," he said to Shawn. "I better get down to the dock."

"I'll be right over," Shawn said. "You start in twenty minutes."

Most of the Cabin 3 campers were sitting on the dock when Riley got there. Patrick stood up. He gave Riley a sheepish grin. "Heard you joined Eldon in the pukers' club."

"Yeah." Riley shook his head. "I ought to be president of that club after what I went through."

"I was a little queasy myself, but me and Barry probably built up an immunity to that Jersey Chicken after eating it every night."

"Don't mention Jersey Chicken," Riley said, laughing. "Ever."

Barry rapped his fist on the dock. "Look who's coming," he said.

They all turned toward the path. The Cabin 4 people were on their way down. They'd be doing the qualifying swim at the same time as Riley's group.

"Remember," Barry said, "we have no idea who messed up our cabin."

"Ghosts," Vinnie said flatly.

"The spirits," Hernando said, holding back a laugh.

Cabin 4's apparent leader—a muscular guy with dark skin and squinty eyes—walked onto the dock and nodded to Barry.

"Afternoon, Kelvin," Barry said, all friendly.

"Heard you boys had a bit of an incident at your cabin the other day," Kelvin said.

"Where'd you hear that?" Barry asked, gazing out at the water.

"Around."

Barry shook his head and licked his lips. "Strangest thing I ever saw," he said softly. "Otherworldly. As if we'd been singled out by a poltergeist."

"Weird stuff," Kelvin said.

"Beyond weird." Barry shook his head. "I had a bad feeling when we got assigned to Cabin 3. I remember last year. . . . Looks like it's happening again."

Before the guy could respond, Shawn and another counselor stepped onto the dock. "You got two minutes," Shawn said. "How many swimmers?"

Eight people from Riley's cabin and nine from the other raised their hands.

"You non-swimmers will ride with the counselors," Shawn said. "Put on life jackets and get in the rowboats. Everybody else line up along the edge of the dock. No contact with any other swimmer or you'll be disqualified."

Barry smirked. "I was planning to dunk a few of those jerks," he said under his breath. "Guess I'll have to wait till the water-polo match."

Riley stared out at the lake. He wasn't sick anymore, just nervous. That turnaround buoy was a long way out.

"The twenty fastest out of all six cabins qualify," said one of the counselors. "There were some quick times in the first group, just so you know."

The counselor blew a whistle and the seventeen

swimmers plunged off the dock. Riley did a shallow racing dive and took a few strokes of the crawl before settling into the breaststroke. That was his most comfortable stroke, and even though it wasn't as quick as the crawl, he figured he ought to gauge his energy level before going all out.

Several swimmers sprinted to the lead, including Vinnie and Colin from Cabin 3. Riley eased over to the side to avoid their splashing feet, falling in behind one of the rowboats.

The water was cool and smelled of vegetation; there were some thick green patches of "seaweed" here and there.

Riley wondered where he'd need to place in this group in order to qualify. The first two cabins had finished earlier, and last year's champion—Duncan Alvarez of Cabin 1—had been more than a minute ahead of the next closest. But then there'd been a pack. So all Riley could do was swim strong and finish strong. There were two more cabins to go later in the afternoon.

Within five minutes Riley had caught a few of the swimmers who'd gone out too fast, including Barry and Hernando. But there were still a half dozen kids out front. The leader—Kelvin from Cabin 4—had fifty yards on Riley and looked relaxed. They were almost halfway to the buoy.

Stick with the breaststroke until the turnaround, Riley told himself. He'd kick it in if he had the strength. So far, last night's illness didn't seem to be affecting him.

The day was overcast but warm, and the sun peeked through every few minutes and then went behind a cloud. There was a breeze blowing straight at the swimmers as they headed up the lake, causing a few chops in the water.

Eldon was just ahead, and Riley took some quick overhand strokes to pull alongside him. Eldon glanced over and spit out some water.

"You good?" Riley asked.

"Little cramp in my side. You?"

"I'm good. Switch to breast till the cramp goes away."

"Okay."

Riley gradually pulled away from Eldon and inched closer to Colin and a swimmer from the other cabin. As they approached the buoy, Riley picked up the pace.

Vinnie, coming toward Riley now on the way back to the dock, called, "Go get 'em, Night Crawler."

Riley quickly raised his fist. "You too." But the leader was at least fifty yards ahead of Vinnie and looking strong. Vinnie was locked in a battle for second with Tony and another swimmer.

Colin, the quiet Cabin 3 kid with lean muscles and very short hair, was right next to Riley as they rounded the buoy. "Let's work together and drop this guy," Colin said, jutting his chin toward the Cabin 4 swimmer who was a yard or so ahead.

It was the first time Riley could remember Colin speaking to him.

Riley took a glance back. Eldon was just making the turn, and three other swimmers were within a few yards of him. So there were at least seven swimmers in contention for fifth place.

Riley had figured that a top-five finish would almost certainly qualify him for the final. There were three heats and twenty qualifying spots, so the law of averages said six or seven from each race would advance.

The sun broke through again and the wind picked up, and Riley noticed a shadow moving through the water a few yards off to his right. He felt a chill and a surge of adrenaline and fear. The water was dark, and visibility through it was nearly zero, but something big definitely seemed to be hovering near the surface.

Riley kept stroking but turned his head hard to watch that spot. Whatever it'd been was already gone. He switched to the crawl and moved faster to get away from that area as quickly as he could.

After thirty yards of hard swimming, Riley had moved into fifth place. If that had been Big Joe, there were now at least a few more swimmers in his domain. Lots of fingers and toes to choose from.

That burst of speed hadn't been a good idea as far as

Riley's racing was concerned. He was puffing now, out of that smooth rhythm he'd developed, and there was a long way to go.

He switched back to breaststroke, lifted his head, and unleashed a loud burp. Then he turned his head and heaved up a large mouthful of orange and brown puke. Peanut butter and Ritz. He swiped at the glob and it quickly spread across the surface of the lake.

Riley kept stroking. The closest rescue boat was about twenty yards behind him, following Eldon's group. Riley had no need to be rescued, but he didn't want to be pulled from the race against his will just because of a little vomit.

"That's nasty!" shouted Colin. "You got puke on my shoulder."

"Dive under," Riley called back. "It'll wash off."

Riley didn't feel very sick, but he was still gasping for air. Colin and the Cabin 4 swimmer caught up and gave him some hard looks. Then they started pulling away.

By the time he was three-quarters of the way to the dock, Riley had regained his breath and settled back into his rhythm. But he was in seventh place, about ten seconds out of sixth and about the same distance ahead of eighth. He could hold that position, but would it be enough? He didn't have much energy left for a sprint.

He could see the swimmers ahead of him—the leader

had a sizable gap on Vinnie and Tony, but the fourth-place swimmer was definitely struggling. Riley knew he'd have been able to catch him if he were feeling right, but today he'd just better try to hang on to the spot he had. Colin and the other kid were closing the gap on that guy, however.

Two counselors in a rowboat moved rapidly toward the fading swimmer. By the time they reached him, Riley had caught him, too.

"You done?" asked a counselor.

The kid shook his head. "Just low on gas," he said. "I'll be fine."

Riley swam to the right to stay clear as he moved into sixth place. "Hang in there," he said.

"You too," the kid replied.

They were less than a hundred yards from the dock. Riley turned and could see Eldon coming strong. He was fifteen yards back but was stroking with everything he had.

Riley continued with the breaststroke, keeping his face down most of the time. Every muscle was aching now.

Eldon was his teammate, but Riley knew every place counted at this point. Beating Eldon could mean the difference between qualifying or not. So he dug as deep as he could and found a little something more. Eldon got closer but Riley held him off and reached the dock a couple of strokes ahead.

He barely had the strength to climb out of the water. He crawled to the edge of the dock and lay flat on his back, too tired to move.

He lay there for at least ten minutes. By then the next two cabins were gathering for their qualifying race. Shawn stepped over to him and poked him in the arm with his toes.

"You okay?" Shawn asked.

"I will be."

"You need anything?"

"Dinner."

"It's two-thirty. Dinner is three hours away."

"I'm starving."

"Come on, then. Let's go see Mrs. Doherty."

"Who's that?"

"She's in charge of the mess hall. Responsible for all those delectable meals we've been eating."

Riley was pretty sure Shawn was being sarcastic, but at this point he'd eat anything.

"Think I qualified?" Riley asked as they walked up the path.

"Looks pretty good," Shawn said. "You and Eldon are twelfth and thirteenth so far. Depends how the next heat goes."

When they got to the mess hall, they went in the back way. Riley'd never been in the kitchen.

"Hello, Mrs. Doherty," Shawn said. "Riley here is in need of sustenance."

"He is, is he?" Mrs. Doherty was an overweight woman in her sixties with dyed-blond hair. She looked Riley up and down and pinched his arm. "Mighty skinny."

"And drained," Shawn said. "He caught a bug last night and couldn't keep anything down. Now he's famished."

Riley nodded. "That's true."

"Well," she said, "dinner is meat loaf, but it isn't near ready. We've got leftover tuna fish from lunch."

Riley just looked at Shawn.

"Maybe something a little less pungent," Shawn said. "A turkey sandwich? Or chicken?" He smiled at Riley. "*Plain* chicken."

Mrs. Doherty opened a large refrigerator and took out a plastic container. She pulled off the lid and showed Riley the contents. "This was supposed to be *my* supper," she said. "From home. A pork chop, mashed potatoes, peas, and gravy. You want it?"

Riley's eyes grew wide as he nodded quickly. "That'd be great."

"My husband made that last night." She put the container in the microwave and shook her head with a smile. "Guess it'll be meat loaf for me."

"I sure appreciate it," Riley said.

"I know you will."

Riley felt like he hadn't eaten in a week. He gobbled down the food and sat for a few minutes, watching Mrs. Doherty and her assistant prepare dinner for the fifty-nine other campers. He might be hungry enough to have some of that later. But for now, he was full and exhausted.

He had two hours of free time ahead. He planned to spend it lying in his bunk.

CAMP OLYMPIA BULLETIN
Friday, August 6

ALVAREZ LEADS 20 INTO BIG SWIM FINAL

Defending Champion Sets Record

Cabin 1's Duncan Alvarez led all qualifiers for the Lake Surprise Showdown, setting a record of 22 minutes, 44 seconds, for the three-quarter-mile trial.

Alvarez is the defending Showdown champion, winning last year's race in 38:09.

The Cabin 3 Threshers had five qualifiers, more than any other cabin.

The 1.2-mile Showdown takes place a week from today—the final evening of camp. We'll have a light early supper that night, with the swimming marathon set for 7:20 p.m. A chicken barbecue and marshmallow roast will follow.

Qualifying Results
(Swimmers in **boldface** advance to the final.)

HEAT 1 (Cabins 1, 2)
1. **Duncan Alvarez (1) 22:44**
2. **Jerry Irwin (1) 24:16**
3. **Ryan McDonald (2) 24:19**
4. **Nigel Singh (2) 24:23**
5. **Omar Ventura (2) 25:09**
6. **Mark Shields (1) 25:49**
7. Jason Sullivan (2) 26:22
8. Jorge Medina (1) 26:29

9. Dennis Chan (2) 26:31
10. Peter Mickelson (1) 27:04

HEAT 2 (Cabins 3, 4)
1. **Kelvin Dawkins (4) 24:22**
2. **Vinnie Kazmerski (3) 24:47**
3. **Tony Maniglia (3) 24:58**
4. **Colin Dugan (3) 25:28**
5. **Malik Rivera (4) 26:02**
6. **Riley Liston (3) 26:21**
7. **Eldon Johnson (3) 26:24**
8. A. J. Castillo (4) 26:42
9. Tom Foley (4) 27:12
10. Barry Monahan (3) 27:20

HEAT 3 (Cabins 5, 6)
1. **Danny Avila (5) 23:53**
2. **Avery Moretti (6) 24:17**
3. **Johnny Rios (5) 24:26**
4. **Troy Hiller (6) 25:42**
5. **Lionel Robertson (6) 26:18**
6. George Macey (5) 26:34
7. Eddie Zevon (5) 27:13
8. Hector Mateo (6) 27:31
9. Rory Hiller (6) 27:38
10. Marc Goldman (5) 27:52

Today's Events

Morning free-throw contest
Afternoon water polo
Evening softball
Sloppy joes for dinner! With ketchup!

CHAPTER SEVEN
The Double Dunk

*B*arry Monahan stared at the Bulletin, slowly shaking his head. "I was twenty-seventh fastest!" he said. "That's what . . . only fifty-two seconds faster and I would have made it."

"Tough break," said Vinnie, bending the paper toward him to take a closer look.

"The dream is over," Barry said, flopping down on his bunk. "Can you imagine how unprecedented it would have been for the hot-dog-eating champion to also qualify for the marathon?"

"Truly Olympian," said Vinnie.

Riley sat on his own bunk and looked at his copy. Ten swimmers had broken twenty-five minutes, and Riley thought he could have at least gone that fast if it hadn't been for his stomach problems. Top ten out of the entire camp would be a huge accomplishment if he could pull it off. And since the final was a considerably longer race, he was pretty sure he could place that high. The longer, the better.

Riley figured being wrenched out and dehydrated had to have cost him a minute, the Big Joe scare slowed him a bit more, and throwing up in the water wasted a little time, too. On a good night, he could definitely move up.

"Training," Barry was saying. "If I'd trained hard instead of sitting on my butt all summer, I would have qualified."

"Yeah," Vinnie said, "that's a heck of a big *if*. You've never trained for anything in your life."

"Not quite true," Barry said. "I trained for the hot-dog contest. Lots of eating. Quickly, too."

Riley stepped outside and stretched his arms high over his head. They were scheduled for a water-polo game in a few minutes—the showdown with Cabin 4—but Riley was thinking ahead to after the game. The big race was still a week away; he had time for some training. He'd be sure to do some laps in the swimming area this afternoon.

Exhausted, Riley sank gently beneath the water, letting his body hang limp for a few seconds before rising to the surface. The ball had gone over the goal and out of bounds, and they were waiting for someone to retrieve it.

Cabin 3 was clinging to a 3–2 lead, and Riley had played most of the game. It'd been intense, with fierce scrambling for the ball and rough play that saw players constantly being dunked and elbowed. Riley couldn't wait for it to end; just a few more minutes and it would be over.

"I hate these guys," Barry mumbled, staring across the water. He'd been playing goalie the entire second half, and he'd made several key saves. Riley had been a big factor, too, helping to slow the Cabin 4 assault.

A counselor dropped the ball in front of Barry, and he passed it to Riley. As usual, two Cabin 4 players scooted toward him. Riley swam sideways and flicked the ball ahead to Vinnie, who was also quickly surrounded.

Riley did a head count: Cabin 4 had only seven players out there, just as Cabin 3 did, but somehow there seemed to be more of them. Or, with the game about to end, maybe they were just more frantic.

"Control the ball!" Barry yelled. "Kill some time."

Head up, Riley swam toward the center, protecting the area in front of the goal and providing a safety valve for a backward pass. Vinnie was underwater, held down by Kelvin Dawkins. The ball shot straight up and Vinnie emerged. Four players slapped at the ball, and it landed three yards in front of Riley.

With a couple of fast strokes he was on it, but he had no time to react before Kelvin pushed him under. Riley hugged the ball to his chest, but there was no way out of this without releasing it. Where would it go? Back toward Barry?

Riley drew his legs in and kicked hard, pushing the ball forward as he broke free. He backstroked underwater and broke through the surface, searching for the ball. Hernando had it, but Kelvin had two hands on his shoulders and a second opponent was coming up from behind.

As Hernando went under, Kelvin grabbed the ball and tossed it to a teammate who was rapidly approaching the Cabin 3 goal. Eldon swam up to meet him, but a return pass found Kelvin wide open. Barry had no chance to stop the shot. The game was tied.

"That was a double dunk!" Hernando called, punching at the water.

"It *was*!" yelled Barry. "How'd you miss that, ref?"

"Looked fair to me," said the counselor who was officiating.

"You're blind," said Barry.

"And you're out of the game!" the counselor said. "Unsportsmanlike conduct."

Shawn clapped and said, "Let's go, Barry. Out of the water."

Barry shook his head and climbed onto the dock. "That was *clearly* a double dunk," he said. "Hernando had two guys putting him under."

The counselor blew his whistle hard. "Time's up," he said.

Riley looked straight up at the clouds, treading water. It sure was frustrating to be tied just as the game ended.

"Clear the water, except for the Cabin Three goalie and one Cabin Four player," the official said. "That violation brings about a penalty shot."

"The double dunk?" Barry asked.

"No. Your whining."

Riley and his teammates stared at the counselor in disbelief. Shawn put Vinnie in goal. Kelvin stayed in the water to take the penalty shot for Cabin 4.

"This is *un*believable," Barry said, standing with his hands on his hips and shaking his head.

Riley stood there dripping. Kelvin took the ball five yards in front of Vinnie, feinted left, then right, and fired the ball toward the upper corner of the goal.

Vinnie strained and stretched. The ball glanced off his arm and into the goal.

Cabin 3 had lost.

Kelvin's teammates dove into the water and mobbed him as Vinnie climbed dejectedly onto the dock.

"We got robbed," Barry said.

"Just shut up!" his brother, Patrick, said. "Don't get yourself suspended from the next game, too."

Vinnie came over now. He punched his thigh with his fist. "We had those guys beat!"

"They cheat, then they get rewarded with a penalty shot," Barry said. "Hernando should've been taking that shot. He was the one that got fouled."

With that, Barry walked quickly away from the water and headed for the cabin, with Vinnie and Patrick and Hernando trailing behind.

Riley looked at Tony, who just shrugged.

"Still want to swim some laps?" Tony asked.

"I'm wiped out," Riley said.

"That's the best time to train. That's how you get stronger. When you're already spent."

"Well, I'm definitely there," Riley said.

"You know what they say. When the going gets tough?"

"Yell at the officials?"

Tony laughed. "Right. The tough get going."

Riley took a deep breath and let it out. "Give me two minutes to rest," he said.

"Okay. Six times to the ropes and back ought to do it, right?"

"I guess."

"Fast as we can go," Tony said. "That race is one week away. I plan to be ready for it. You too?"

Riley closed his eyes and nodded. "Let's make it eight laps," he said. "I think we need all the training we can get."

CAMP OLYMPIA BULLETIN

Saturday, August 7

SURPRISE WINNER IN FREE-THROW CONTEST

Rios Edges Robertson in Final-Round Shoot-out

Johnny Rios of Cabin 5 emerged as the surprise winner of the free-throw contest yesterday morning, hitting 9 out of 10 shots in the final round to edge sharp-shooting Lionel Robertson (Cabin 6), who made 8. Robertson had made 16 of 20 shots in the preliminary rounds.

Vinnie Kazmerski (Cabin 3) and Danny Avila (5) tied for third, with Kelvin Dawkins (4) in fifth.

Water-Polo Action Heats Up

Close contests were the norm Friday afternoon at the Aquatics Center, with Cabins 1, 4, and 5 scoring one-goal victories. The scores: Wonders 3, Tubers 2; Fortunes 4, Threshers 3; Fighters 2, Sixers 1.

In softball, it was Sixers 9, Fortunes 4; Threshers 7, Wonders 3; and Fighters 8, Tubers 4.

Standings

Basketball	W	L
Cabin 4	3	1
Cabin 5	3	1
Cabin 1	2	2
Cabin 3	2	2
Cabin 2	1	3
Cabin 6	1	3

Softball	W	L
Cabin 3	3	0
Cabin 5	2	1
Cabin 1	1	2
Cabin 2	1	2
Cabin 4	1	2
Cabin 6	1	2

Water Polo	W	L
Cabin 4	3	1
Cabin 3	3	1
Cabin 2	2	2
Cabin 1	2	2
Cabin 5	1	3
Cabin 6	1	3

CHAPTER EIGHT
Perfect Aim

"*Tonight,*" Barry said, sitting on his bunk and looking seriously from camper to camper, "Cabin Four gets what's coming to them. Eleven hundred and fifty hours."

"That's lunchtime," Tony said. "You mean twenty-three hundred and fifty."

"Whatever. Just before midnight. The witching hour."

That was just over an hour away. Riley was lying in his bunk, but he was on top of his sleeping bag and was still dressed. Like most of the others, his flashlight was on and was turned faceup to point toward the ceiling. There was no other light source in the cabins, so this was the usual routine before lights-out.

Barry made it clear that at least four people had to stay behind.

"If we're all gone at once, it'll arouse too much suspicion," he said. "Patrick, Kirby, Colin, and Diego stay put. Make it seem like we're all in the cabin somehow—laugh a lot and say things like, 'Quit acting like a baby, Tony!' or, 'Hernando, your socks stink!'"

"They do not," Hernando said. "My mom packed enough so I'd have fresh ones every day."

"That's beside the point," Barry said. "I want people to think you're in the cabin."

"What about you?"

"Me too. They can say, 'Barry, you are a very cool guy.'"

"Or they can say, 'Barry, you sure have a fat butt.'"

"Whatever. Now everybody else follow me. Quietly."

Riley figured he'd been chosen because he was fast, not because he was suddenly popular with these guys. He couldn't see the plan working anyway.

Barry had explained that they'd hide in the woods near Cabin 4—"With absolute silence," he demanded—until the campers had settled in for the night. Then they'd begin to toss pinecones or pebbles onto the roof of the cabin. Just a few, just to set a mood that not everything was peaceful outside.

"Wow," said Tony. "Pebbles on the roof. What could be scarier than that?"

"Listen, wise guy!" Barry said. "That's just the start. We do that a couple of times, then we stay quiet for ten or fifteen minutes. Then we do it again."

"Ooh. They'll be thinking, *There must be a ghost on the roof now.*"

"It's just to set the atmosphere," Barry said. "Make them *slightly* uneasy. So when the real fun starts, they're already sort of agitated."

"And what's the 'real fun'?" Hernando asked. "Bigger pebbles?"

Barry smiled and folded his arms. "Eggs."

"Eggs?" asked Hernando. "What's scary about eggs?"

Barry reached under his bunk and pulled out an egg carton. He opened it to show that it held seven eggs. "I found these in the Dumpster behind the mess hall," he said. "They must be rotten or they wouldn't be throwing them out."

"They must be *totally* rotten," Eldon said, "or they'd be serving them for breakfast tomorrow."

"Exactly," Barry said. "These are a couple of weeks past their expiration date. When the time is right, I'll throw one at the door of their cabin. They'll come out to see what's going on, then all six of us will let them have it."

"I still don't see what's scary about that," Hernando said.

"It doesn't *have* to be scary," Barry said. "It'll be gross and they'll never know who did it."

"How won't they know?"

"It'll be dark. And we'll be hiding. And we'll be *very* quiet, got it?"

Riley looked from face to face. Hernando and Vinnie were grinning as if it was the coolest thing they'd ever heard. Eldon and Tony looked as if they thought it was the stupidest.

Barry looked smug and triumphant. "Remember," he said. "No noise. You three—Eldon, Tony, and Night Crawler—head out like you're going to the Larry, then circle through the woods and meet us at the far end of the clearing. There's enough of a moon that you don't need to use your flashlights, but bring 'em anyway. And keep your mouths shut."

Riley followed Tony and Eldon, walking away from the cabins. He had an uneasy feeling that he'd probably be getting beat up by the Cabin 4 guys before the night was over. How would they get back to Cabin 3 without being detected?

"This is beyond ridiculous," Tony said.

"Yeah," said Eldon, "but it *would* be pretty cool if we could pull it off."

"Barry's got his brains in his butt sometimes," Tony said. "But yeah, it'd be sweet if we got away with it."

As they reached the bathhouse, they saw Kelvin from Cabin 4 walking out. "Evening, chumps," he said, stopping on the path.

"Nice job in the contest today," Tony said. Cabin 4 had won the tug-of-war event that morning.

"Thanks. Wore me out."

"Us too," Tony said, yawning widely. "Can't wait to hit the sack. I'm falling asleep just standing here."

Eldon and Riley yawned, too.

"I guess lights-out is any second now," Tony said. "Everybody else from our cabin is already in bed."

Kelvin shrugged. "Yeah, well, whatever. See you boys tomorrow."

They waited until Kelvin was halfway to the cabins. "Good one," Tony said, grinning widely.

Oh yeah, thought Riley, *they'll* never *suspect us now.*

The "lights-out" call came and the three of them ducked into the woods.

Riley swallowed hard. Kelvin seemed like a decent guy, but he was big and strong and could definitely take anybody in Cabin 3. And there'd been enough friction between the two cabins already that they'd be the most likely suspects by about a thousand to one.

Still, this was exciting. They were supposed to be tucked in their bunks, being good Olympians. Instead they were stalking through the dark forest looking for revenge. Riley'd been "behind the scenes" a lot lately: the counselors' cabin before the swim race, the mess hall kitchen after. Now this.

It took at least ten minutes to silently creep across the few hundred yards to the edge of the clearing. They heard

Barry making hooting noises as planned, pretending to be an owl. Tony hooted back, and soon all six of them were kneeling and trying not to laugh. Riley's eyes were fully adjusted to the dark; he could see pretty well.

"I'll keep the eggs in the carton for now," Barry whispered. "Get some little pebbles. And pinecones. When I start moving, you follow me and keep your mouths shut. If you have to sneeze, just suck it up and *don't*. We'll be going slow. This is the last verbal communication you'll get until it's over, so listen up."

Riley sat on the ground and kept his eyes on Barry. They were all dressed in their darkest clothes—Riley had black shorts and a blue sweatshirt that said SEASIDE HEIGHTS. His mom had bought it for him on the boardwalk back in June, when they'd rented a house near the beach for a week.

"I'll throw the stones and things," Barry said. "Just hand them to me one at a time. When I give the signal—I'll put up one finger—then you'll each be given an egg. Spread out so you have perfect aim at the door. I'll do the first throw, then we wait for them to come out. When I whistle"—he let out a swift double tweeting to demonstrate—"we clobber them with eggs. Then retreat quickly and *quietly*."

"To where?" Vinnie asked.

"Deep into the woods. Back to our cabin, eventually. Whatever you do"—Barry pointed at Eldon, then at

Riley—"don't get caught. Under no circumstances can this mission fail. Any wimp that screws this up will be plenty sorry."

Riley gulped again. *Beyond ridiculous*, he thought. But maybe it would work.

They moved to a spot in the woods about thirty-five yards from Cabin 4, which was across the clearing from their own. All six cabins were dark now. Barry opened the egg carton and set it at his feet. He tossed a pebble toward the roof of the cabin and it landed with a *ping*.

There was no reaction, so Barry tossed another one, then a third. A flashlight flicked on in the cabin, then went off. Riley felt a small shudder of triumph. Barry nodded approvingly.

After about three minutes, Barry tossed another pebble, then two more quickly. Kelvin stepped through the doorway and shined his flashlight at the roof, then into the trees above the cabin. He shrugged and went inside.

Riley caught Eldon's eye and they both started laughing silently. Barry whacked Riley across the shoulders—not very hard—then started laughing, too. "Five minutes," he mouthed.

An unfamiliar sound—like a huff or a cough—made them all turn, looking into the deeper woods. *"No flashlights,"* Barry said, barely at a whisper but with great sternness.

They all turned back toward the cabin. Riley looked over his shoulder. He could hear footsteps in the forest. Just a few quiet steps, well spaced, as if someone or something was trying to sneak up.

Riley nudged Eldon and gestured with his head. "Something's out there," he whispered as softly as he could.

Eldon turned, squinting as if that would help him to hear. There was another huff, barely audible. Eldon looked at Riley and nodded.

Barry stood and tossed three more pebbles in quick succession, each one *ping*ing on the roof. He opened the carton of eggs, but all of the boys had turned toward the woods.

Something large was running straight at them; they could hear it crashing through the underbrush. Riley bumped into Hernando as they all tried to scatter, stumbling in the darkness. He felt a quick, sharp pain as his knee hit the ground, but he bounced up and sprinted.

Barry fell flat, crushing the eggs against his chest, as whatever it was galloped past.

They made it to the edge of the clearing, with Barry calling them together with his hooting. His shirt was covered with slimy, rotten egg.

Outside Cabin 4, Kelvin and the others were shining their flashlights and looking around. The Cabin 3 residents stayed huddled in the dark, out of flashlight range. Their only movements were their chests pumping as they tried to catch their breaths.

"Must've been a deer," Riley said after Kelvin and the others had gone in.

"I didn't see no deer," Barry said, shaking his head. "If it was a deer, we'd have seen it. Whatever it was ran within about two inches of us."

"I think it went *through* us," Vinnie said. "I swear, I felt something cold and misty."

"And angry!" Hernando said. "I felt it, too."

"We felt it, we heard it, and we didn't even see it!" Barry said. "What does that tell you?"

"A ghost," said Hernando.

"Maynard!" said Vinnie.

"None other," Barry responded. "That was him."

CAMP OLYMPIA BULLETIN
Sunday, August 8

HALFWAY HOME!

Cabin 5 Leads at Midpoint of Camp

Balanced scoring in contests ranging from free-throw shooting to the tug-of-war have the Fighters in the lead for the Big Joe Trophy with 33 points, but it's a close race from top to bottom. The huge points from basketball, softball, and water polo are yet to be awarded. And the decisive Lake Surprise Showdown on Friday night will test the camp's strongest swimmers in the final event of the season.

Today's feature is the cross-country relay race. Who are the fastest runners in camp?

UP-TO-THE-MINUTE TOTALS

Cabin Five 33; Six 31; One 28; Two 26; Three 25; Four 24

The "Larry Awards"

Cabin 3's resident comedian Barry Monahan has provided us with his mid-camp "Larry Awards." Here's the list, along with his commentary, which he asked us to publish. He did not request police protection.

Worst meal of the week: Sausage pie with creamed broccoli. ("It looked exactly the same when I puked it up two hours later.")

Most disgusting rash: Colin Dugan's. ("Hint: Don't wipe your butt with poison ivy.")

Biggest crime: That last-second penalty shot against us. ("I will appeal to the highest court in the land!")

Worst urinal aim: A multi-camper tie. ("I wish I'd brought my fishing boots.")

Dumbest camp rule: No seconds on anything until you've eaten everything on your plate. ("Please, then—no more road-killed groundhog burgers.")

Most haunted cabins: 3 and 4. ("Something is out to get us!")

CHAPTER NINE
Sprinting the Hill

*R*iley trudged back to the cabin after the softball game, not waiting for anyone else. The whole team had been lacking spirit and energy, and it showed. They'd suffered their first softball loss of the season.

Worse for Riley, he'd made two costly errors in right field and struck out twice. Barry muttered that they'd be better off with no right fielder at all.

None of them had slept very well after the Maynard scare. Riley kept waiting for the cabin door to burst open, with the counselors threatening to kick them out of camp. What had that really been? Too big for a deer, too *invisible*. Riley knew for sure that Big Joe was real. Maynard might be, too.

But the night had passed without any more incidents, and everything had seemed normal at breakfast.

Riley opened his gym bag and took out the letter he'd received from his parents the day before. Nothing special, just a "Hope you're having a fantastic time. We miss you!" and all that. He'd read it ten times already. He kept thinking about the great time they'd had at the beach two months before; about playing basketball with his father in their driveway in Jersey City; about sitting on the front porch with his parents on summer evenings, eating pizza. He couldn't wait to get home, especially after a game like this morning's.

He flopped onto the bunk and shut his eyes. Thinking about that last day of camp—the last night—somehow made it seem as if it would get there faster. When he was swimming laps—imagining himself passing other competitors as they worked their way across the lake—it was as if each stroke brought him closer to home.

He wouldn't be swimming today, though. The cross-country relay was this afternoon, and his cabin mates had identified him as a fast runner with endurance. He'd be running the key next-to-last leg of the race. The longest one.

The one with the most at stake.

The race was to start in front of the mess hall, covering a flat, grassy area for about two hundred yards before dipping down to the water. The teams of runners—eight from each cabin—would run varying distances, circling the lake and finishing back at the starting line.

The afternoon was hot and humid, so the runners had abandoned their T-shirts and were dressed in shorts and sweatbands.

Riley followed a counselor and one runner from each of the other five cabins to a spot on the far side of the lake. They'd be the seventh legs, covering about eight hundred meters—the last third of it up Olympia Hill—and handing off to the anchor legs. Vinnie would be waiting at the top of the hill for the final two-hundred-meter sprint.

The entire race would cover about two and a half miles.

Riley scoped out his competition. Troy Hiller from Cabin 6 looked strong and fast; he'd hit a couple of triples against Riley's team in softball that would have been doubles by a slower runner. And this kid Medina from Cabin 1 was built like a wrestler—lean and wiry, probably very quick.

But Riley knew that by the time the first six runners had finished their legs, the competitors would probably be spread out. So he might be way behind some of these guys before he even started running—or way ahead.

Part of him didn't want to be ahead when he got the stick from Eldon. Squandering the lead would be embarrassing.

A whistle blew far across the lake, and Riley stretched

his neck to see the runners sprinting across the field. Tony Maniglia was leading off for the Threshers. He was easy to spot—taller than the other five runners and darker. He'd moved into second place, but the pack was very tight.

Barry and Hernando were sitting this one out. They were the only paunchy guys in the cabin; everybody else was either skinny like Riley and Eldon or muscular like Vinnie and Diego.

Tony and the others had reached the boat house and were straining to finish. The Cabin 5 runner had a ten-meter lead, but Tony was right in the thick of it with the others. He stumbled as he handed the stick to Diego, but the pass was clean and Diego sprinted onto the path.

They were behind the trees now, and Riley had a hard time keeping track of the racers. It was more than a minute before he got his next clear glimpse, and by then Kirby had the stick. He was in third.

Riley turned back to the guys he'd be running against. Jorge Medina was bouncing up and down, eyes shut, sweat dripping down his chest. Nearby, Troy Hiller had his hands propped against a maple trunk, stretching out his legs. Riley could hear shouts of encouragement from across the lake, but over here things were dead quiet. And tense.

"They're at the bridge!" said one of the runners, a tall guy in a purple headband over a brush cut. Cabin 5. He'd worked his way down to the lakeshore to get a better look. "My team's got the lead. Then three guys packed real tight behind him; couldn't tell who they were."

The kid scrambled up the bank and lined up on the path. "Any minute now," he said.

That would be Patrick running for Cabin 3. Patrick was fast, but Riley wasn't sure how well he'd hold up over a full quarter mile. *Just get the stick to Eldon,* he thought. *Don't blow it, Patrick.*

Riley took a deep breath and let it out, trying to calm himself. But his heart was pumping hard and his breathing was rapid. He shook his wrists and shifted his shoulders from side to side. He could see about a hundred yards down the path, so he'd have a good idea of the situation as Eldon approached.

"That's us!" said the brush-cut guy. A lone runner in a purple headband had rounded the turn and was sprinting toward Riley's group. Two seconds later the Cabin 4 runner emerged, with Eldon and the Cabin 1 racer right on his heels.

This last part of their leg was slightly uphill, and the strain on the runners' faces was evident. Eldon was pumping his arms hard and grimacing, but he was losing ground to the others.

The Cabin 5 runner grabbed the stick from his teammate

and took off hard. Riley stretched his arm back, waiting for the exchange from Eldon. The last two runners were climbing the hill behind him.

"Get 'em!" Eldon shouted as he slid the metal track baton into Riley's palm. Riley gripped it tight—it was lighter than it looked, smooth and hollow, about a foot long. Head up, Riley sprinted along the path.

Settle in, he told himself. *Plenty of time*. He'd be running a half mile, lots of room to make up the deficit. The leader was about twenty meters ahead, and the next two weren't far behind that guy. They were all scrambling for position, probably moving too fast for such a long leg on this very hot afternoon.

The path climbed for about a hundred meters, then dipped closer to the lake. The Cabin 5 runner had extended the lead to twenty-five meters, but Riley had closed slightly on the others.

Coming downhill, Riley glanced back. The two runners trailing him were a good distance behind. But looking back had been a bad move; Riley's right foot hit a rock and he began to fall, leaning way forward and stumbling.

Somehow he managed to keep his footing and remain upright. They'd reached the lake, in full view now of all the other campers. He could hear Barry's voice above the others: "Sprint, Night Crawler! Sprint!"

But Riley knew it was too early to sprint. He was only halfway through his leg. He focused on the two runners ahead of him on the path—Jorge Medina and some kid from Cabin 4. They were running side by side, trying to stay close to the leader and gearing up for a fast finish.

Riley felt good. He *wanted* to sprint now, but he knew he had to save something for that hill. His teammates were watching. Vinnie was up there waiting.

As he rounded a turn and left the path, he could see the three runners ahead of him, churning their arms as they began to climb the hill toward the mess hall. The distance between them had shortened considerably; Riley was close enough to see the streams of sweat inching down their backs and to hear the labor of their breathing.

"Yeah!" shouted Tony, standing on the side of the hill and pumping his fists. "You got 'em, Riley! Dig down!"

Hernando was at the top of the hill, near the anchor runners. "Come *on*, Liston!" he called, leaning forward with two fists. "These guys are dying!"

With his focus on Medina, Riley barely noticed that they were passing the purple-headband guy, who had slowed to nearly a walk. And the Cabin 4 runner was clutching at his side as Riley sprinted past. Now Riley was neck and neck with Medina, just fifty meters from the exchange point.

Suddenly the air before him was clear; Riley'd passed all

of them and was dashing toward Vinnie. He could see the scowl on the Cabin 1 anchor's face as his team lost the lead. And Cabin 4's Kelvin Dawkins was a picture of determination, waiting to sprint that final two hundred meters. Vinnie'd be in for a battle.

Riley got there first. Vinnie took the baton and raced toward the mess hall. There was no room for strategy now—this was an all-out sprint to the finish.

Riley stopped cold and shut his eyes. Medina barreled into him from behind and Riley dropped to his knees. "Sorry," Medina said, puffing hard.

"No problem."

Medina yanked him to his feet and they watched as Kelvin Dawkins rapidly made up ground on Vinnie. The guy had to be the fastest runner in camp.

But Riley had given Vinnie a ten-meter lead, just enough to make all the difference. Vinnie finished inches in front, lifting his arms overhead and shouting, "Yes!"

Barry was running toward Vinnie—the only running Barry would do today—with Hernando and Tony right behind. Riley flopped to the grass and stretched out on his back, huffing and sweating and cramping.

He sat up and pulled in his knees, wrapping his arms around them and letting his chin sink to his chest. The sun felt good; his breathing was getting back to normal. Kirby and Diego had made their way over now and were running up the hill toward Barry and the others, pumping their fists and shouting.

Vinnie would get all the credit for holding off Dawkins, but Riley knew the score. He'd made all the difference in that race. He'd been the man.

That had been truly Olympian.

CAMP OLYMPIA BULLETIN
Monday, August 9

IT'S CHAMPIONSHIP TIME!

Play-offs in Major Sports Begin Tomorrow

Semifinals in basketball kick off a frantic four days of championship action Tuesday, culminating in the awarding of the Big Joe Trophy on Friday night.

Top-seeded Cabin 4 meets Cabin 1 in the first semifinal. It'll be Cabin 5 against Cabin 3 in the other.

Points in the major sports are 50 for the champions and 25 for the runners-up, so the Big Joe standings can change quickly. The third-place team gets 15, fourth is worth 10, and fifth earns 5.

Softball semifinals are Wednesday morning and water-polo semis are Thursday. The championship games in each sport are as follows:

Basketball: 8:30 p.m. Wednesday
Softball: 1 p.m. Thursday
Water polo: 11:30 a.m. Friday

Cabin 3 Runs Off with Relay

Cabin 3's Vinnie Kazmerski held off Cabin 4's fast-closing Kelvin Dawkins to win the round-the-lake cross-country relay race Sunday afternoon. Cabin 3 moved from fourth place to first on the next-to-last leg.

Cabin 1 finished a close third.

Quote of the Day

"It was like climbing Mount Everest with a backpack full of rocks and a knife plunging into your lungs." —*Cabin 1's Jorge Medina after racing up Olympia Hill*

CHAPTER TEN
Like the Loch Ness Monster

*B*y late Monday afternoon, Cabin 3 had won its last regular-season games in softball and water polo, securing high seeds in the play-offs for both sports.

Barry and Colin were competing in the archery contest, but nobody else even wanted to watch.

"Let's hit the yacht club," Tony said. So Riley followed several of his cabin mates down toward the water.

"You bring a fishing pole?" Tony asked him.

Riley shook his head. "Don't have one."

"You can use one of mine. You want to?"

Riley's face brightened. "Yeah." Nobody'd asked him to go fishing the whole time he'd been at camp.

"Grab the tackle box," Tony said. "I'll get a boat."

Eldon and Riley sat side by side in the back of the rowboat and Tony took the oars, rowing across the lake. The morning had been very hot and humid, but things had turned overcast as the afternoon wore on. The wind was picking up.

"This is better fishing weather," Eldon said, looking up at the clouds. "The fish don't bite when the sun's strong."

The lake was dotted with canoes and rowboats. "I caught a good-sized bass the other day out by the totem pole," Tony said. "Let's head there."

The totem pole sat on a tiny island near the farthest edge of the lake. It was about ten feet tall, with a huge eagle's head carved on top.

"You guys know how to row?" Tony asked, turning his head.

Eldon shrugged. Riley said, "No."

"It's easy. Switch spots with me."

Carefully, Eldon and Riley moved up as Tony shifted back, each keeping a hand on the side of the boat. Riley put both hands on an oar and Eldon took the other.

Riley's oar skipped along the surface and the metal oar-lock rattled. The boat began turning toward the left.

"In sync, guys," Tony said. "You have to row in unison."

After a minute or so they straightened things out and began to move forward.

"This is the spot," Tony said. He handed Riley a fishing rod. "You know how to cast?"

"Yeah. I've been fishing a few times." With his dad. He'd never caught anything, though, not even a bluegill or a catfish.

Riley looked at the lure on the end of his line, a fat yellow orb with black spots.

"That's my best bass plug," Tony said. "It worked great last time I was out here."

Riley cast the lure as hard as he could, but it landed only about fifteen feet from the boat. Eldon and Tony cast to the other side.

"You hear about Cabin Five?" Tony asked.

"What about 'em?"

"Somebody poured soda or lemonade all over the floor of the cabin yesterday afternoon. By the time they got back from the relay, there were about ten trillion ants."

Eldon and Riley laughed. "They know who did it?" Eldon asked.

"They think it was somebody from Cabin One. But the Cabin Five guys are the ones who had to deal with it."

There was a low rumble of thunder way in the distance. The counselors would call in the boats if there was any chance of a storm. There were still a few breaks in the clouds, though; a couple of rays of sun were peeking through.

"I heard a good one," Eldon said. "When Cabin Two was

playing water polo the other day, somebody snuck into their cabin and tied all the sneakers together by the laces."

Tony gave a short laugh. "Pretty good, but not as clever as the lemonade."

"Guess not."

Riley reeled in his line and checked the lure. They hadn't had any bites yet. He cast it better this time. "Pretty deep out here?" he asked.

Tony scrunched up his face as if he was thinking hard. "I saw a depth chart once at the Trading Post. I think it gets forty feet deep in a few spots."

"We'll be out here *without* a boat in a few days," Riley said.

"You know it."

The qualifying heats for the swim marathon hadn't taken them this far out, but the final race would. Riley looked back toward the dock. It was a *long* way to swim.

"It'll be intense," Tony said. "Out here in all this water, night coming on . . . Tell you what, my strategy is gonna be to do my fastest swimming right around here. Get to the turnaround point and sprint my butt back home."

Riley laughed. "Don't want to be another Maynard."

"You got that right."

They were the only boat out this far; it was at least a couple of hundred yards to the nearest canoe. Riley felt a drop of rain on his neck. The sky was all clouds now.

"Hope Big Joe will be sleeping Friday evening," Eldon said with a grin. "Going to be a lot of commotion out here, with twenty guys racing through."

"It's not just him you have to worry about," Tony said. "I heard somebody saying there's a *Little* Joe, too. And the only reason they call him Little is because he's smaller than Big Joe. But not by much."

"How old is Big Joe supposed to be anyway?" Eldon asked. "Like a hundred?"

Tony shrugged. "Nobody knows. Snapping turtles live a long, long time. And they never stop growing."

Riley heard more thunder and glanced at the sky. But then he felt a hard tug on his fishing pole. The line was stretched tight and the tip of the rod was bending toward the water.

"You got one!" Tony yelled. "Looks big."

"Reel him in!" Eldon shouted.

Riley started reeling, and the line zigzagged through the water. Eldon and Tony brought their lines in and Tony picked up the net.

The fish was at the surface now, thrashing the water about ten feet from the boat and pulling hard. It dove under, but they'd had a good look at it.

"That's a nice bass," Tony said. "Give him a little line to play with."

"Why?" Riley asked, reeling even harder.

Suddenly the line went limp.

"That's why," Tony said. "That was a big, strong fish. You needed to let him tire himself out a bit before bringing him in."

Riley brought in the empty line.

"So much for my favorite plug," Tony said with a sigh.

"I'll pay you for it."

"Nah."

Lightning flashed, and a shrill whistle sounded from the dock. A counselor was waving an orange flag and continuing to blow the whistle. Another counselor with a megaphone was calling, "All boats in!"

"Let's hustle!" Tony said. "Me and Eldon. Let's go."

So Riley moved to the back again and Eldon and Tony began rowing. Small waves were smacking against the boat, and the thunder sounded much closer. The rain was steady now but light.

Something to the right—maybe twenty yards from the boat—caught Riley's eye. A grayish head, about the size of a football, was sticking up from the lake. "That's him!" Riley shouted.

"Wow!" said Eldon as he and Tony stopped rowing.

They could see a hint of grayish green shell beneath the water. And then the creature was gone, slipping below the surface and out of sight.

"Big Joe," Tony said, his mouth open and his eyes wide.

"Definitely," Riley said. "I'm pretty sure I saw him under the water during the swim race. But there's no question that was him just now."

The whistle blew again, and the counselor with the megaphone demanded that all boats return. Tony and Eldon picked up the oars and started rowing harder.

Riley kept staring at that spot on the lake as it receded in the distance. He'd only half believed those stories before. He'd *wanted* to think that a giant snapper could live in a lake like this, undisturbed for more than a century, offering an occasional glimpse of himself to worried campers. Like the Loch Ness Monster or Bigfoot. Now Riley'd seen it for himself.

"Too bad we didn't have a camera," Tony said.

"That's what everybody says," Eldon replied. "Nobody's ever caught that thing on film. That why it's legendary."

They were quiet now as they moved smoothly across the lake. The rain increased and soaked their shirts, but none of them cared.

Riley looked up a few times when lightning flashed, but he wasn't scared. The thrill of seeing that turtle had him elated.

They were nearly to the dock when the counselor blew his whistle again. "Move, boys!" he yelled harshly. It was the same counselor who'd cost them the water-polo game with his last-second penalty call.

Tony steered the boat to the dock. "We *are* moving," he grumbled. Coming to a stop, he set his tackle box and the fishing rods on the dock.

"Out of the boat!" the counselor said. "We've been calling you in for twenty minutes. You have to *listen* when you're out that far."

"We heard you," Tony said. "We were all the way on the other side."

"I could ban you from the water for the rest of the week!"

"We got back here as fast as we could."

Riley couldn't contain his excitement. "We saw Big Joe!"

The counselor scowled. "Sure you did."

"It was definitely one of the Joes," Tony said. "Way out by the totem pole."

The counselor shook his head. "Listen, this camp's been in business for twenty-seven years. Thousands of kids have swum in this lake; we do the across-the-lake race every summer. You think we could get away with having a giant turtle biting people's feet off? Some lawyer would put us out of business in two seconds."

"We saw it," Riley said firmly.

The counselor's voice softened a little, but not much. "There's some big fish in this lake. Once in a while a carp'll break the surface, especially during a storm. That's what you saw. If anything."

Riley looked back across the lake. All of the boats were in now, and the rain was pelting down on the surface. There were even some waves breaking against the dock.

He'd keep his mouth shut. But he knew what he'd seen. That'd been a turtle. A *big* one.

CAMP OLYMPIA BULLETIN

Tuesday, August 10

CABIN 5 CLINGS TO OVERALL LEAD

Zevon Triumphant in Bow-and-Arrow Blitz

Eddie Zevon of Cabin 5 emerged as the winner of Monday's archery contest, hitting two bull's-eyes and coming close with two other shots. Troy Hiller (6) was second, with Omar Ventura (2) third.

Zevon's points helped Cabin 5 hold on to its narrow lead in the points race with 53, but Cabin 3 has moved up to second with 52 on the strength of Sunday's cross-country win. The other cabins are tightly bunched behind.

Major points will be awarded Wednesday, Thursday, and Friday in basketball, softball, and water polo.

Play-off Schedule

Tonight: Basketball
Semifinals, 7 p.m.: 1 vs. 4 followed by 3 vs. 5

Wednesday: Basketball
Fifth-place game (2 vs. 6), 2 p.m.
Third-place game, 4 p.m.
Championship, 8:30 p.m.

Wednesday: Softball
Semifinals, 9 a.m.: 1 vs. 3 followed by 2 vs. 5

Thursday: Softball
Fifth-place game (4 vs. 6), 9 a.m.
Third-place game, 10:30 a.m.
Championship, 1 p.m.

Thursday: Water polo
Semifinals, 3:30 p.m.: 2 vs. 6 followed by 3 vs. 4

Friday: Water polo
Fifth-place game (1 vs. 5), 9 a.m.
Third-place game, 10:15 a.m.
Championship, 11:30 a.m.

CHAPTER ELEVEN
Air Ball!

"*L*ooks to me like we've taken the lead," Barry said, climbing out of the lake and slapping hands with his teammates. "That's fifteen points right there."

Cabin 3 had just won the eight-man swimming relay, with each camper covering one length of the water-polo area.

"And we're the only team that made the semis in all three major sports," Vinnie announced. "That Big Joe Trophy is going home with us!"

Riley shook some water off his arms and smiled. He'd raced a strong seventh leg, maintaining the lead. He was well suited for these speed and endurance events. The strength and accuracy games like basketball and softball were where he stunk.

They all knew that the trophy would actually be staying here at camp, but CABIN 3—JERSEY CITY, NJ would be engraved on it for this season if they won. The winning team members would all be going home with gold-colored medals, just like in the real Olympics, with silver medals for second place and bronze for third.

Bringing home a gold medal would be cool.

"Now we rest up for tonight," Barry said. Their semifinal basketball game would be a rematch with Cabin 5, which had trounced them a week earlier. "We are *rolling* now. Nobody's gonna slow us down."

Riley groaned as he made his way up the lunch line. It was make-your-own-sandwich day, but the main offerings were bologna and cheese. The cheese looked hard and dried out. He opted for peanut butter again.

"Gross," said Eldon, who was next in line. "Guess we're supposed to live on candy bars from the Trading Post."

"At least they have bananas today." Riley scooped a small amount of salad onto his plate, too.

They found seats at the end of one of the tables, then went back for "grape drink," which seemed more like purple sugar water.

Eldon looked at his plate and winced. "What was it the brochure said? 'Lavish and healthy dining options at every meal'?" He shook his head slowly. "We'd be better off foraging for acorns in the forest."

Riley took a bite of his sandwich. He'd had peanut butter at least once every day so far, but he didn't really mind. He ate it that often at home, too.

Barry and Vinnie and Hernando were one table over, laughing and flicking bits of bologna at each other.

"They never stop, do they?" Eldon said. He began breaking his cheese hunk into smaller squares and stacking them up.

Riley shrugged. "They're happy guys," he said with a bit of sarcasm.

Eldon's cheese stack was about two inches tall now, and he topped it with a hunk of cucumber. "Spectacular," he said.

"You should be an architect."

"I might."

"Think we'll win tonight?"

Eldon looked across the mess hall, then back at Riley. "They killed us last time. Who knows?" He frowned and picked a thin slice of tomato from his plate, holding it up to the light. "It's not even red. It's like a mushy pink. Isn't August supposed to be prime tomato season?"

"I don't think 'prime' is the right word for anything that comes out of that kitchen," Riley said. He took a big mouthful of grape drink, then stood to get a refill. "A few more days of this. As soon as we get home, my parents said they'd take me to Burger King. You want to come with us?"

"Definitely."

Halftime. Cabin 3 held a 21–18 lead, and everyone had played their required quarter except Riley.

"Think you can handle Rios?" Shawn asked. He had a worried look. Vinnie and Tony were both in foul trouble.

Johnny Rios was the best shooter in camp. Riley looked out at the court, where Rios and the other Cabin 5 players were warming up for the second half. Riley nodded. "Maybe."

Shawn laughed. "That's what I like to see. Such great confidence." He put his hand on Riley's shoulder. "I'll tell the other guys to try to help you out, but that team has a lot of weapons. Rios is the only one near your height. Everybody else would smother you."

Riley gulped. Quarters only lasted eight minutes. *Just keep the ball away from me*, he thought. *And away from Rios.*

But Cabin 5 spotted the mismatch immediately and Rios went to work. He drove for a layup on the first possession and lost Riley with a head fake on the second, swishing a short jumper.

"*Cover* him!" Barry urged as they ran up the court.

Riley looked away. He moved toward the corner, with Rios all over him. No way they'd be passing to Riley.

Cabin 5 extended the lead to three points a minute later. And as they ran back, Rios didn't even bother covering Riley. He double-teamed whoever had the ball, and Colin eventually made an errant pass that went out of bounds.

Seconds later, Rios hit a three-pointer. Cabin 3 hadn't scored since halftime.

Barry called a time-out. "He's killing you," he said as he walked past Riley, shaking his head.

Riley didn't say a word. What did they expect? The guy was like an NBA all-star.

"Barry, you'll have to switch to Rios," Shawn said in the huddle. "Take his man, Riley. He's got about fifty pounds on you, but he's slow. Just box him out and try to keep him away from the basket."

"Thanks a lot," Barry muttered to Riley as they walked back onto the court. "Now I gotta run my butt off chasing Rios because you can't cover *any*body."

Cabin 5 stuck with its defensive matchups, with Rios running free and nobody covering Riley. So Riley was wide open, and Tony tossed him the ball.

Riley had a clear shot at the basket, but he was way beyond the three-point line. He dribbled twice and Rios darted over. Riley grabbed the ball with both hands and turned his body, but Rios slapped it loose and shoved him out of the way.

The whistle blew. Riley'd been fouled. He wouldn't be shooting, but at least Cabin 3 was getting the ball back.

Tony walked over to Riley and leaned toward his ear. "Next time he lunges at you, get a shot off," he said. "If he fouls you again, at least you'll go to the line."

Riley nodded. He hadn't scored a single point this season. Maybe he could make a free throw.

Vinnie finally scored, but Cabin 3 was four points behind. Rios hit another three-pointer, leaving Barry stumbling backward.

Tony brought the ball up and drove toward the basket, stopping at the baseline as Rios and another defender blocked his path. Riley had followed the play and was alone in the corner. Tony flipped him the ball and yelled, "Shoot!"

The ball slipped out of Riley's hands and he reached for it, turning his shoulder toward the basket. As he turned back, he saw Rios leaping toward him. So he shot.

Rios's hand whacked Riley hard on the shoulder and his momentum sent them both to the floor. The whistle blew again.

"Foul on number seven, purple," the referee said. "Five orange shoots three."

Riley glanced at the scoreboard. Less than two minutes remained in the quarter. Cabin 5 was up, 30–23.

"You can put us right back in it," Tony said, grabbing Riley's arm.

"You *owe* us," Barry said. He ran both hands over his face, which was dripping with sweat.

Riley stepped to the line. He'd made just three out of ten in the free-throw contest last week. His hands were shaking.

"Nice and easy!" Shawn called.

Riley let out his breath and stared at the basket.

His first shot hit the back of the rim, rolled to the side, and fell out. Barry groaned. Vinnie clapped and said, "Two more, Night Crawler."

Riley shut his eyes quickly, then caught the ball. He crouched slightly, lifted the ball to forehead level, and released. This time it kissed the front of the rim and fell in. Riley felt a big surge of excitement. He watched the scoreboard as the 23 turned to 24.

"All right! All right," Barry said, shaking a fist.

"Another one," said Hernando.

But Riley's third shot didn't even reach the basket. The Cabin 5 bench erupted with shouts of "Air ball!"

Riley cursed silently and trotted back to play defense.

Barry didn't fare any better than Riley had. Rios added a layup and a fallaway jumper before the buzzer sounded, giving him fourteen points in the third quarter alone.

Riley sat on the bench with his arms folded tightly for the entire fourth quarter. His teammates were steaming mad when the game ended. They'd lost by twenty-two.

Can't blame all that on me, Riley thought. But that didn't make him feel any better. How could they ever win gold medals after a performance like that?

CAMP OLYMPIA BULLETIN
Wednesday, August 11

BASKETBALL CHAMPIONSHIP TONIGHT

Fighters and Fortunes Will Vie for Title

Johnny Rios pumped in a season-high 27 points as the Cabin 5 Fighters thrashed the Cabin 3 Threshers, 51–29, to advance to the basketball title game. The Cabin 4 Fortunes also qualified, edging the Cabin 1 Wonders, 38–35, as Kelvin Dawkins scored 15.

Play-off pandemonium continues today with softball semi-finals this morning and basketball consolation games this afternoon. A full house is expected at the Arena for tonight's basketball final.

End-of-Season T-shirt Sale at Trading Post

Commemorate a sensational two weeks of sports action with a Camp Olympia T-shirt that you can wear all year. Regularly selling for $15, a selection of shirts has been marked down to $13.50 for this week only.

The sky-blue style is available in XL and XXL, and the "gold medal" yellow model is available in all sizes except M and L.

The popular dark blue T-shirts are still available at the regular price. They make cherished gifts for parents, friends, and siblings!

CHAPTER TWELVE
Shooting Stars

*T*his is so boring, Riley thought, sitting on the top row of the bleachers at the basketball championship. Most of his cabin mates were a couple of rows below him, shoving each other and whooping and not paying any attention to the game.

Barry and Vinnie were acting pretty full of themselves, having sparked a far better day for Cabin 3. They'd moved into the softball final with an 8–3 win in the morning, then stormed back to take third place in basketball in the afternoon.

Riley hadn't done much in either game. He'd drawn a walk and grounded out a couple of times in softball and played an uneventful third quarter of the basketball game, barely touching the ball.

He figured no one would notice if he slipped out of the

gym at halftime. He walked slowly down the creaky old bleachers and out the door.

It was after nine o'clock, so it was fully dark out. Lots of stars were overhead, and the half-moon was coming up over the lake. Riley headed toward it.

Just about everybody was at the basketball game, so things were quiet out here. Riley walked down the hill, flicking on his flashlight.

Just a few more days and he'd be home. Back to eating his parents' cooking, sleeping in his own bed in his own room, showering in private.

In less than three weeks he'd be back at school.

Camp hadn't been so bad. He'd become friends with Eldon and Tony, and even Barry and Vinnie and Hernando hadn't treated him badly. Just some teasing and the occasional frustration when he screwed up in sports, and he could live with that.

Besides, everybody was weak at something. Barry and Hernando were useless in endurance events like swimming and running, and Vinnie had done poorly in the canoe race and had fallen down during the tug-of-war.

Still, those guys and Tony had carried the team in basketball and softball, and they'd all played well in water polo. Riley hadn't made any big impact except for that leg in the relay race, and that had gone mostly unnoticed.

He had one huge opportunity ahead of him, though.

He'd been swimming laps for a half hour every day, mostly with Tony and sometimes with Eldon. A few times he'd seen other kids practicing, but nobody had done as much swimming as he had.

He stopped by the water and looked across the lake, all the way down to the totem pole.

Could he win it? He could dream about it, but it seemed impossible. He'd studied the results of the trials in the Bulletin, and a top-ten finish seemed within his reach. But the best swimmers were just too far out there.

Riley shut his eyes and took a deep breath, bringing in the smell of the lake. Crickets were chirping, and he could hear the occasional bellow of a frog. The air was still and moist, but he was wearing a light sweatshirt, more for comfort than warmth.

He felt like he could swim that race right now, cutting through the cool water, biding his time in the middle of the pack, making a big move midway through and reeling in the guys who went out too fast.

He'd gain strength as the race wore on, stroking past swimmers who were gasping for air and desperately trying to hang on. Then that all-out sprint, picking off one or two others in the final fifty meters as his teammates went wild on the dock.

He swallowed. His heart was pumping hard now, and all he'd been doing was *thinking* about the race.

Two more days. Less than that, even. Race time was forty-six hours away.

He walked past the boat house and onto the path that circled the lake. Had eleven days really passed since the last time he walked this loop alone at night? In some ways it seemed like forever, and in other ways it seemed like yesterday.

He'd been scared that first night, wondering if he'd make it back or wind up lost in the woods. He'd been embarrassed, too, after getting scorched in the basketball game and having Barry mock him about girls. So he'd been dreading the two weeks ahead.

He wasn't scared anymore. Being on this path tonight felt comfortable; he knew the way now. There was nothing more to dread. Friday night's race would be his breakthrough.

Something broke the water with a splash, and Riley turned his light toward it. Nothing remained but a spreading ring of ripples. Probably a bass. Maybe the one he'd hooked.

Way back up the hill he could see a line of flashlights moving toward the cabins. The basketball game must have ended. Barry had invited some guys from Cabin 1 over for a poker tournament, but Riley didn't care about missing it.

He was almost to the end of the lake now, but he was in no hurry to head back. He climbed atop a large flat boulder that jutted a few feet into the water and spread out on his back. He shut off his flashlight and looked up at the stars.

There were millions of them. He lay on that rock for nearly an hour, just looking at the constellations. Somewhere nearby Big Joe must be resting. Riley felt comfortable being in his presence. Two creatures out here alone, not bothering anybody. Just being self-reliant. Independent.

Suddenly an intense streak of light caught his eye. A shooting star. It made a rapid arc, then burned out as quickly as it had appeared.

Riley remembered what Shawn had told them about the Perseid meteor shower, which occurred in mid-August every year. Apparently it was under way.

A second meteor appeared a few minutes later, smaller than the first. Every few minutes Riley would see another one, usually lasting no more than a second.

Cool, he thought. *Everybody else is missing this.*

Shawn had said the shower would be most intense after midnight, but Riley wouldn't be staying up that late. A few more minutes; that would be plenty.

When he got up to leave, the moon was higher in the sky and the natural light was nearly enough to see by. But he decided to make the full loop around the lake instead of heading back the way he came, and it was still pretty dark in the woods. So he used his flashlight.

He crossed the bridge and walked faster. He wanted to tell Tony and Eldon to get outside and see the Perseids. They'd appreciate it. Maybe some of the others would, too. Maybe even Patrick.

As he rounded a turn, he realized that he was nearly to the point where he'd taken the baton in that relay race. This was the hill where Eldon had started to falter, leaving Riley with some ground to make up on the three runners ahead of him.

Riley started jogging, carefully lighting the path. When he reached the top of the hill, his heart was pumping; it was as if that race was going on all over again.

He ran down the hill where he'd stumbled in daylight, this time keeping his balance and beginning to move faster. There was better visibility as he came off the slope, just a bit of light from the boat house across the way.

The flashlight felt like a baton in his hand. He imagined those other runners just ahead of him straining and puffing while he felt so fresh. He burst out of the woods and began climbing Olympia Hill, pumping his arms and nearly sprinting already, feeling like a champion, feeling stronger than he'd ever been in his life.

He was running faster than he had in that relay, but it

felt almost effortless. Past the top of the hill; he'd finish this race now. He'd take on that final sprint to the mess hall.

After the work of climbing the hill, this flat stretch felt like nothing. Riley poured it on, top speed all the way until he reached the dark space beyond the finish line.

He walked now, sweating and breathing deeply. He raised his arms overhead, feeling triumphant.

Slowly he made his way back toward the cabins. A few lights were on, and he could hear some kids laughing. Three or four guys were gathered around a campfire outside Cabin 2.

He stopped near the Larry, scanning the sky again. He waited a couple of minutes but didn't see any more meteors.

Down the hill Lake Surprise was lit by the moon. It looked deep and cool and peaceful.

A great home for a giant snapping turtle. And a great place for a swimming marathon.

Riley looked forward to both things connecting.

Two more days. He knew he was ready for anything.

CAMP OLYMPIA BULLETIN

Thursday, August 12

FORTUNES CLAIM HARDWOOD CROWN

Inside Strength Makes the Difference

It was Dawkins over Rios in an exciting and combative basketball final last night. Kelvin Dawkins dominated the boards and scored 18 points as the Fortunes held off the Fighters, 41–37. Johnny Rios continued his hot hand, pouring in 21 points in a losing effort.

Earlier in the day, Cabin 3 claimed third place over Cabin 1, 33–30. Vinnie Kazmerski scored 14 for the Threshers.

Who's Got the Edge for the Big Joe Trophy?

It's too close to call. The Cabin 4 Fortunes have taken an 8-point lead over the Cabin 5 Fighters, 91–83, but the Cabin 3 Threshers are right behind with 82. The Threshers will battle the Fighters in today's softball final, so those standings might be changing significantly.

The water-polo semis are late this afternoon. The Fortunes and Threshers go head to head for one spot in the final, with the Tubers and Sixers vying for the other.

Quote of the Day

"This is the most exciting race for the Big Joe Trophy I've ever witnessed," said counselor Shawn Pearson, who is in his second season on the Camp Olympia staff.

CHAPTER THIRTEEN
A Quick-Rising Storm

*R*iley and Tony swam frantically toward the player with the ball, but the opponent deftly flipped it back to one of his teammates. Vinnie and Hernando sprinted in that direction, but the Cabin 4 players were very effective at keep-away.

Only seconds remained, and the Threshers were trailing by a goal.

"Get the ball!" shouted Barry.

No kidding, Riley thought. But Cabin 4 had controlled the action for several minutes.

Riley and Eldon had moved up from the defensive zone, putting six Threshers on the attack. But when Kelvin Dawkins tossed the ball into an empty corner of the playing area, their fate was sealed. Riley and the others swam back toward it, but the whistle blew before they got there. Game over.

Riley climbed out of the water and sat on the dock in disbelief. It all seemed to be coming apart.

They'd just lost the water-polo semifinal, capping a horrible day for Cabin 3. They hadn't even been close in the softball final earlier in the day, dropping an 11–2 nightmare. Riley'd struck out three times.

"We stunk!" said Barry, staring out at the lake.

"We got trashed," Patrick said, shaking his head.

"Losing to those guys, of all people," Barry said. "The biggest jerks in camp."

Riley looked up as Tony took a seat next to him. "Maybe we should get some more eggs," Tony whispered. Then he grinned.

Riley didn't dare laugh. He'd played poorly in the water-polo game, too, although Barry had let three goals get past him in the second half.

Kelvin and a couple of other Cabin 4 players hopped out of the water in front of Riley's team. "Looks like that trophy's gonna be ours," Kelvin said, flexing his muscles.

"We're still mathematically alive," Barry said defiantly. "We scored big points for that second place in softball, and we can salvage third in water polo tomorrow."

"Sure," Kelvin said. "Third place is right where you guys belong."

Barry stepped closer to Kelvin and stared him straight in the face. "I'm talking about *first* place, my friend. You haven't sewn up anything yet."

"You better call the Ghostbusters," Kelvin said as he started to walk away. "No way you can overtake us by yourselves."

"We'll see," Barry said, turning to his teammates. "It's not over yet."

"Yeah," said Vinnie. "Anyway, I'm starving. It's dinnertime."

"How can you think of eating after a loss like that?" Barry asked.

"Still gotta eat."

"Not me," Barry said. "I'm too agitated. . . . What's on the menu?"

"Chicken," said Hernando.

"Real chicken?"

"Of course not. Some chicken-like substance in gravy."

"Okay," Barry said. "I'll eat. But I'm calling a team meeting for tonight. Nine-thirty at the trash barrel. Don't be late. This is crunch time."

Riley walked up the hill with Eldon and Tony.

"Can we really still win this thing?" Eldon asked.

Tony shrugged. "If we all swim out of our minds tomorrow night, maybe. I mean, we'd have to do *much* better than we did in qualifying. But it's possible. We sure didn't help our cause today."

They'd dragged a fallen tree trunk out of the woods and set it near the barrel, so Riley sat on it with Eldon, Kirby, and Diego. The others stood around the fire or sat on the ground. Barry stood behind the barrel and stared silently at the flames for a while before speaking.

"What bothers me the most," he whispered, "is letting Cabin Four get away with that nonsense they did to our cabin last week."

"They're jerks," Hernando said.

"Yeah, they are," Barry replied. "We had the perfect retaliation planned, but then Maynard intervened."

Barry looked from face to face. Vinnie and Patrick nodded sternly.

"It was a brilliant plan," Barry continued, "but there are forces at work in this camp that are beyond human understanding. For some reason, those forces didn't want us to get revenge at that time. I'm at peace with that. These things happen for a reason."

"Amen to that," said Vinnie.

Riley squirmed on the trunk. He could feel the heat from the barrel, but he was too low to see the flames. The sky overhead was as clear and starry as the night before.

"Losing to those guys today was a big setback," Barry said, "but I've studied this carefully. As long as we win the consolation game tomorrow, we'll still be very much in the hunt, no matter what happens in the championship. It'll all come down to the swimming, and I'm expecting Tony and Vinnie to have outstanding races. If Colin and you others can pick up a few points, then we might just pull this off."

Riley took a deep breath and let it out slowly. Eldon caught his eye and smirked. They were "you others," but Riley didn't mind that he hadn't been mentioned by name. He didn't need any more pressure.

"The sweetest revenge is victory," Barry said. "That's the message. Straight from Maynard and whatever other spirits had a hand in all this. If we win that Big Joe Trophy, those Cabin Four guys can kiss my butt."

"You said it!" Vinnie shouted.

"You're the man!" added Hernando.

"I am," Barry said. "We are. Tomorrow night we'll be champions."

They all stared at the barrel for a minute before Patrick asked, "Meeting over?"

"Meeting over," Barry said. "But this fire'll be burning for a few hours if anybody wants to stick around."

Vinnie and Tony and some others wandered off. Riley and Eldon and Diego stood and stepped up to the barrel.

Barry put his hands in his pockets and looked at the sky. He pulled a small bag of M&M's from his pocket and passed it around. Riley took two red ones and a green one and popped them into his mouth.

Barry swept his hand in the direction that Vinnie and Tony and Colin had gone. "I'm glad they took off," he said. "I didn't want to disturb them, but something happened last night that might be repeated. I wouldn't want to freak them out about swimming across the lake."

The bag came back to Barry and he emptied the last of the M&M's into his mouth, then tossed the wrapper into the barrel. He slowly chewed the candies, then cleared his throat.

"I couldn't sleep last night—too keyed up about today's games—so I walked down by the lake. It was way after midnight, probably one or one-thirty.

"I was past the boat house, headed for that extra-dark area where the light can't get through the treetops. There's no sound at all; everybody in camp is dead asleep and there's not a single light on anywhere. I stop walking and just look out at the lake. There's not even a ripple of a wave. Everything's still."

Barry looked at his arm and scratched a mosquito bite, then went back to staring into the fire. He nodded very gently a few times, as if pondering what to say next.

"I don't know if any of you guys ever heard this—they keep real quiet about it around here—but maybe forty years ago a canoe tipped over in that lake at night. It was one of those quick-rising storms like we had a few days ago, and these guys—they were just a little older than we are—got swamped by a wave. Or by something. Or some*one*. I think it was Maynard. They were way out in the deepest section, fishing for bass. A couple of hundred yards from any shoreline.

"Nobody wore life jackets back then. And these guys couldn't swim. Nobody even knew they were out there; it was before this was a camp. It was just a lake in the woods.

"So, needless to say, they all disappeared. The canoe washed up on the shore, but nobody ever found a trace of those guys. Not a sneaker or a skull or anything."

Riley swallowed hard. Barry caught his eye and looked down.

"So I'm standing there last night, minding my own business, and I see this *very* faint blue light coming toward me from the lake. It's three separate lights actually, but they're not lighting anything up, you know? Just these forms floating toward me above the surface of the water. And as they get closer, I see that it's three people, and they're moving really slowly, but they're frantically stroking with their arms and churning their legs, as if they're trying to sprint as hard as they can, but they're barely getting anywhere.

"But they *do* keep moving toward me, clawing at the air. And as they're getting closer, I can tell that they're kids—kids our age—and they're choking and gasping but not making a sound.

"It's those drowning guys, desperately trying to get away from the lake and failing. They get twenty yards from shore, and then they vanish. I see the blue lights sinking under the water and a bigger *violet* light rising from below. And when I get a clear look at it, it's a guy with a giant hole ripped through his throat."

Barry bit down on his lip and slowly shook his head. He started to speak, then stopped. He looked around the circle, first at Eldon, then at Kirby, Diego, and Riley.

"Yeah, Maynard. And those three kids," he said, his voice dropping again to a whisper. "They must be stuck there, constantly trying to save themselves and never quite making it. Forty years those kids've been struggling. Can you imagine that?"

Riley's mouth was hanging open and his lips were dry from the heat. He licked them and shivered, then inched closer to the fire. Nobody said anything for a long time.

"Think Big Joe ate 'em?" Eldon asked.

Barry shut his eyes quickly and nodded. "Why not? They were dead, right? Might as well make a meal out of 'em. They had no use for their bodies."

"Not even a trace of them, huh?" Diego asked.

"Not even a trace." Barry stretched his arms over his head and yawned. "Any of you guys want to wander down there later . . . Well, maybe it's a once-a-year thing. Who knows? *I* ain't going back, but . . . that lake is a powerful place."

Riley nodded. No one seemed eager to go down there, and he certainly didn't need to. He yawned. He was tired. They all were. But nobody moved. They stood by the fire for another half hour, just watching as it burned down to the embers.

CAMP OLYMPIA BULLETIN
Special Edition

Dinnertime
Friday, August 13

DAWKINS NAMED CAMP MVP

All-Stars Selected in Major Sports

Johnny Rios, Danny Avila, Lionel Robertson, Tony Maniglia, and Vinnie Kazmerski have each nabbed spots on two all-star teams along with the camp's Most Valuable Player, Kelvin Dawkins of Cabin 4.

Dawkins led his team to the basketball and water-polo titles. Earlier in camp, he won his section of the swim-marathon qualifier, helped his cabin to victory in the tug-of-war, and was a high finisher in free-throw shooting.

The Stars

Softball	Basketball	Water Polo
1B: B. Monahan (3)	G: Rios (5)	Goalie: Rivera (4)
2B: Rios (5)	G: Dawkins (4)	Forward: Dawkins (4)
3B: Castillo (4)	F: Avila (5)	F: Alvarez (1)
SS: Maniglia (3)	F: Shields (1)	F: Kazmerski (3)
P: Avila (5)	C: Robertson (6)	F: Maniglia (3)
C: Robertson (6)		Defense: Singh (2)
OF: Kazmerski (3)		D: T. Hiller (6)
OF: Sullivan (2)		
OF: Medina (1)		

Cabin 4 Holds Lead; Fighters Poised for Victory

Cabin 4's second major championship of the season this afternoon vaulted them into the lead for the Big Joe Trophy. The Fortunes knocked off the Tubers to win the water-polo championship, 3–1. But with only the swimming marathon remaining to be contested, second-place Cabin 5 has an excellent chance to claim the overall crown.

Based on the qualifying races, Cabin 4's only realistic hope for big points tonight is Kelvin Dawkins. Cabin 5 has a couple of contenders in Danny Avila and Johnny Rios.

Cabin 3 sits in third place after winning the water-polo consolation match this morning. With five qualifiers for tonight's swim—more than any other cabin—the Threshers have an outside shot at the title.

Defending champion Duncan Alvarez of Cabin 1 is the favorite to win the individual championship.

Big Joe Standings

Cabin 4 146 points
Cabin 5 138
Cabin 3 122
Cabin 2 79
Cabin 1 70
Cabin 6 62

187 points still up for grabs!

Tonight's winner will score 30 points for his cabin, with the runner-up gaining 25 and third place nabbing 20. The top fifteen places count.

Here's the allocation, starting with first place:
30 25 20 18 16 14 12 10 9 8 7 6 5 4 3

Who's got the Camp Olympia spirit?

CHAPTER FOURTEEN
Truly Olympian

*I*n the minutes before the race, Riley couldn't keep still. *Steady your breathing,* he kept telling himself, but it was no use.

He glanced around the dock at the other swimmers. Duncan Alvarez looked so strong and confident. Why wouldn't he? He'd won this race last summer and was the overwhelming favorite to repeat.

And then there were guys like Danny Avila and Avery Moretti. They looked like men compared to Riley, with muscular shoulders and square jaws and scowls.

Riley's own teammates were equally quiet. Vinnie was pacing the dock; Tony was sitting with his legs dangling in the water, rapidly drumming his thighs with his fists. Eldon and Colin looked scared.

A counselor picked up a megaphone and said, "Two

minutes, boys. Any physical contact with another swimmer will mean immediate disqualification. There are counselors in rowboats about every hundred meters." He gestured toward the water. There was a long string of boats leading all the way to the totem pole. "If you get in trouble, just raise your arms overhead and tread water. There are roving canoes out there, too, so you'll be rescued within seconds. Any questions?"

No one said anything.

Riley shut his eyes and took a few deep breaths. His fingers were tingling from nervousness, and sweat was dripping down his face. He unwrapped his orange headband from his wrist and pulled it down toward his ears.

Suck it up, he thought. *This is what you've been working toward. You want this.*

He stared across the lake. There was more of a breeze tonight, but nothing much to speak of. It'd be in their faces on the way out. The sun was setting behind them, but there'd be plenty of light for at least another hour.

"Go, Cabin Three!" Barry hollered from the shore. The non-swimmers weren't allowed on the dock until the race was under way.

"Do it up, Kelvin!" came another shout. The spectators all began yelling.

The counselor stepped to the side of the dock and raised

his arm. "Ready," he said. "Get set." He blew his whistle sharply and Riley and the others dove off the dock.

His urge to sprint was almost uncontrollable, but that would be lethal at this point. *Settle down*, he thought. This race was almost twice as long as the trials.

Riley stayed with the crawl in the early going, knowing that he could switch to the breaststroke whenever he needed a breather. For now, he needed to stay in contact with the pack.

He could already tell that some swimmers were starting too fast. Within a minute he was twenty meters behind the leader, and only three swimmers were in back of him. But the biggest group was just a few strokes ahead, including Vinnie and Tony.

"That's Avery Moretti with the early lead," came an announcement over the loudspeaker. "The defending champion is right with him."

The water in front of Riley was all churned up by the many kicking feet. He counted nine swimmers immediately ahead of him, spread out over four or five meters. Colin was just to Riley's left, and basketball star Johnny Rios was to his right.

You're in contention, Riley thought. *Long way to go. Be patient.*

He decided to shut out the distractions for a few minutes

and just swim comfortably before assessing whether to make a move. So he put his head down and moved steadily, counting fifty strokes with each arm before looking ahead.

Rios remained beside him, and the line of swimmers in front had stretched out a bit. Moretti appeared to be holding on to the lead, but Alvarez was still with him. There was a small gap to the next group of three and then a bigger space, and all but those five leaders were still within striking distance.

Vinnie and Tony were in that next group. Riley and Rios were eleventh and twelfth at the moment, but they were just a couple of strokes ahead of Colin and the next bunch.

You're way ahead of last time, he thought. *No puking in the water tonight.*

By the time they reached the yellow buoy where they'd turned around in the trials, Riley and Rios had joined the large group that included Vinnie and Tony. There were eight of them now. Everyone looked steady; no one was struggling yet. He was the smallest one in this pack by far.

They were still about a quarter mile from the midpoint of the race. The five swimmers out front were way ahead of them.

Nearly everybody in Riley's group had finished at least a minute faster than he had in the qualifying heats. Now he was right here with them, and he was feeling great. He knew he was riding the edge and that fatigue could overtake him anytime, but he'd never wanted anything more than to hang in there and beat some of these people.

He switched to the breaststroke for a few minutes, steadying his breathing. Everyone was swimming hard, but no one was making any decisive moves just yet. It was a battle of endurance for now.

Before long he heard another announcement: "Moretti continues to lead at the midpoint, with Alvarez a body length behind. Both swimmers are well under record pace."

As the leaders passed him heading for home, Riley counted the seconds between them and the next group of three. There was at least a twenty-second gap. Kelvin Dawkins was right in the mix.

That trio was a good minute ahead of Riley's pack, which still included eight swimmers. Several of them picked up the pace as they neared the turnaround point. Riley swung wide and passed Troy Hiller and Omar Ventura, moving into tenth for the moment.

Homestretch, Riley thought. *Halfway there! Top ten is yours for the taking.*

The next group was coming toward them now, still heading for the turn. Riley looked for his teammates. He spotted Colin in a pack of four. Eldon had moved up and joined him. They were more than a minute behind Riley but very much in contention for some points.

"Cabin Three!" Riley called.

"Looking good!" Eldon yelled back.

The exchange with Eldon gave him a lift. *Time to make a move,* he thought. *String out this pack and see who's a real contender.*

He quickly found himself abreast of Vinnie and Tony. Vinnie looked shocked when he noticed Riley, but then he grinned. "Where'd you come from, Liston?"

"I've been right behind you the whole race," Riley said, his words coming in between puffs.

"We can do this," Tony said. "Big points if we hold these spots. More if we can pick off a few guys."

Cabin 2 teammates Ryan McDonald and Nigel Singh were just ahead of them, so the trio from Cabin 3 was sitting 8-9-10, with Johnny Rios a half stroke back. Ventura and Hiller were beginning to slip farther behind. It was a long way ahead to the leaders.

Work with these guys, Riley told himself. *Forget about the top five. The race is right here.*

If he could drop one more swimmer, he'd be assured of a top-ten finish. And despite being tired, he still felt awesome. No cramps, no pain. They were all doing the breaststroke now, saving energy for the final push.

Fifteen more minutes and this would be over. Riley could already see the yellow buoy up ahead.

The breeze had shifted and was blowing across the lake, coming from the swimmers' left. A shadow to his right caught Riley's attention, a darker spot in the water that seemed to be moving toward them.

"Big Joe!" he said.

Tony and Vinnie looked over. Riley tightened his stroke, bringing his arms closer to his body and his legs up to the surface. He watched the spot as he moved away from it.

"Watch your toes," Vinnie said, smiling.

Whatever had been there was gone, but it had left Riley with a new surge of adrenaline. This lake really was magical. He could feel its energy coursing through him.

Riley didn't buy Barry's story about Maynard or those other ghosts haunting the lake. There was no negative energy in here—just a legendary giant snapper. A real one.

By the time they reached the yellow buoy, they'd caught Singh and McDonald.

"How you holding up?" Vinnie asked Riley.

"Holding up great."

"Tony?"

"I'm okay."

"Let's drop these chumps," Vinnie said. He put his head down and returned to the crawl. Riley and Tony did, too.

They swam harder for about two minutes, staying together. When Riley looked back, McDonald was fifteen meters behind. But Rios and Singh were still in contention.

This is it now, Riley thought. The ten hardest minutes of his life, but it'd be worth it. He could feel Big Joe's presence, but he wasn't scared. Just excited.

He stayed tucked behind Vinnie and Tony, enduring as well as he could as the five swimmers churned through the water. He felt another surge of enthusiasm as Singh suddenly dropped off the pace.

Rios stroked hard and pulled alongside Tony. He wasn't yielding at all. Riley'd been with him since the opening seconds, but now Rios was pouring it on.

Riley could see Barry and Hernando and the others up on the dock, about three hundred meters away. A lone swimmer was approaching the finish line, and a tight group of four was battling for the next places.

Another announcement rang out over the lake: "Alvarez is way ahead of record pace. Let's make some noise and bring him home!"

So Moretti had faltered. Would he hold on for second? Riley couldn't tell what was going on in the pack up ahead.

Everyone in his group was straining now. Each stroke brought them closer.

"Big points!" Vinnie gasped. "Hang in, Riley."

Riley's arms were heavy now. His heart was pounding against his ribs.

He glanced back quickly. Several swimmers were still within striking distance. Any letup would definitely cost him a few places.

But no one was pulling away. Vinnie and Tony and Rios were still right there, an arm's distance from him, hoping to reserve just enough strength for a kick. Riley knew he probably couldn't out-sprint any of them over a very short distance. But maybe he could make them work just enough to exhaust them, to rob any kick they might have left.

He'd been cautious enough. Now it was time to move. He counted twenty hard strokes with each arm, then popped his head up. He'd moved ahead, just a meter or so, but all three seemed to be breathing even harder. They'd had to work to keep up with him. Riley was in sixth place.

Breathe, he told himself. *Keep stroking.*

Again he surged. Another count of twenty. Still they were with him, but nobody was talking anymore.

Now he could hear Barry yelling. He could see Patrick and Hernando pumping their fists, less than one hundred meters away.

And just ahead in the water, struggling mightily, was a swimmer in a red headband. Moretti. He was perhaps twenty meters in front of Riley, but he'd had a gap of well over a minute not long before.

One more surge, Riley thought. These guys would be going all out over the final fifty meters. He needed to build a lead.

It hurt. It hurt worse than anything he'd ever experienced. But he'd never had so much at stake. This wasn't about the team; it was about him.

He inched ahead. The water was noisy now—Vinnie and Tony and Rios churning behind him, the spectators yelling, Riley's own breath coming in loud, shallow huffs.

"Sprint!" Was that Barry yelling or was it all in Riley's head? It didn't matter now. Sprinting was all he could do.

Moretti was right there. Fifth place could be Riley's. His arms and legs were burning now, his stomach muscles twitching.

Everything, he yelled inside. *Every ounce you've got!*

Moretti surged. Riley rose out of the water, reaching for the dock. His hands hit it first. He'd done it.

He shut his eyes and sank beneath the water. When he emerged, he watched Tony and then Vinnie grab the next two spots.

It took him forever to climb out of the water. Barry came over and smacked him on the shoulder. "Fantastic job, Night Crawler."

"Did we win it?" Riley gasped.

"Too close to tell."

Riley smacked hands with Eldon, who had sprinted in for fifteenth, the final scoring position. Then he walked to the far end of the dock, away from everybody else.

Twilight. Up the hill he could see smoke from the barbecue pit. Across the lake the totem pole was catching the dwindling rays of the sun. The last few swimmers were approaching the finish line, with several rowboats trailing behind.

Maybe they'd won it; he'd know soon enough. A gold medal would be nice, but it would be nothing compared to fifth place in the Showdown. *That* he'd earned by himself. As an athlete.

He'd come a long way since that qualifying race. Tonight he'd knocked off a dozen guys who were clearly expected to beat him.

Riley took a last long look at the lake.

Then he headed for the barbecue.

Maybe next year he'd come back and win it all.

CAMP OLYMPIA BULLETIN
Final Edition
Saturday, August 14

CABIN 3 WINS BIG JOE TROPHY

Late Surge by Swimmers Makes the Difference

The Threshers ran up 49 points on the strength of four top-ten finishers in the Lake Surprise Showdown, moving from third place to the top of the standings in the final event of camp.

Led by Riley Liston's surprising fifth-place finish, the Threshers added points from Tony Maniglia (7th), Vinnie Kazmerski (8th), Colin Dugan (10th), and Eldon Johnson (15th).

Duncan Alvarez defended his title, smashing the camp record in 36:54. Cabin 1 had the first two finishers and the last two.

Final Big Joe Standings

Cabin 3 171 points
Cabin 4 166
Cabin 5 165
Cabin 1 125
Cabin 2 96
Cabin 6 81

Lake Surprise Showdown Results

1. Duncan Alvarez (Cabin 1) 36:54
2. Jerry Irwin (1) 38:31
3. Kelvin Dawkins (4) 38:35
4. Danny Avila (5) 38:37
5. Riley Liston (3) 39:16
6. Avery Moretti (6) 39:17
7. Tony Maniglia (3) 39:21
8. Vinnie Kazmerski (3) 39:22
9. Johnny Rios (5) 39:24
10. Colin Dugan (3) 40:35

11. Nigel Singh (2) 40:37
12. Ryan McDonald (2) 40:40
13. Lionel Robertson (6) 41:01
14. Omar Ventura (2) 41:48
15. Eldon Johnson (3) 42:33
16. Malik Rivera (4) 42:36
17. Troy Hiller (6) 42:41
18. Jorge Medina (1) 43:18
19. Mark Shields (1) 43:22
— Jason Sullivan (2) did not finish

About the Author

Rich Wallace is the acclaimed author of many books for young readers, including *Perpetual Check; One Good Punch,* an ALA-YALSA Best Book for Young Adults; *Wrestling Sturbridge,* an ALA Top Ten Best Book for Young Adults; and *Shots on Goal,* a *Booklist* Top 10 Youth Sports Book. At age eleven, he spent two weeks at Camp Aheka in New Jersey, where he swam a mile in Surprise Lake, home of a legendary giant snapping turtle named Big Joe.

Rich Wallace lives in New Hampshire with his wife, author Sandra Neil Wallace. You can visit him on the Web at www.richwallacebooks.com.